STARING OUT AT THEM WAS THE EVIL, GRINNING
FACE OF THE CHINESE WARRIOR.

Terror at Moaning Cliff   *Frontispiece (Page 226)*

MELODY LANE MYSTERY STORIES

TERROR AT MOANING CLIFF

BY

LILIAN GARIS

Author of

THE GHOST OF MELODY LANE,
THE TOWER SECRET,
NANCY BRANDON'S MYSTERY,
THE WILD WARNING, ETC.

GROSSET & DUNLAP
PUBLISHERS   NEW YORK

BOOKS BY LILIAN GARIS

MELODY LANE MYSTERY STORIES

THE GHOST OF MELODY LANE
THE FORBIDDEN TRAIL
THE TOWER SECRET
THE WILD WARNING
TERROR AT MOANING CLIFF

Mystery Stories for Girls

GLORIA: A GIRL AND HER DAD
GLORIA AT BOARDING SCHOOL
JOAN: JUST GIRL
JOAN'S GARDEN OF ADVENTURE
CONNIE LORING
CONNIE LORING'S GYPSY FRIEND
BARBARA HALE
BARBARA HALE'S MYSTERY FRIEND
CLEO'S MISTY RAINBOW
CLEO'S CONQUEST
NANCY BRANDON
NANCY BRANDON'S MYSTERY
A GIRL CALLED TED
TED AND TONY
SALLY FOR SHORT
SALLY FOUND OUT
JUDY JORDAN
JUDY JORDAN'S DISCOVERY

To
SALLY IGOE
Who sends me such lovely messages

CONTENTS

vii

CONTENTS

TERROR AT MOANING CLIFF

CHAPTER I

A MYSTERIOUS LETTER

THE two sisters, Carol and Cecy Duncan, were so excited they could scarcely talk, and this was serious, at least for Cecy. The girls were helping their father, Felix Duncan, pack for a hurried trip to a business convention. In the midst of these preparations the carrier had left, with the other mail, a most unexpected and strange letter from Aunt Isabel Duncan—Mr. Duncan's aunt, really, but the letter was for Carol.

"What did she say?" whispered Cecy, as she was stuffing some socks into a spare pair of her father's shoes; for Carol had said this helped to keep the shoes in shape almost as well as trees, and wasn't nearly so heavy. "What did Aunt Isabel say?" Cecy repeated her whisper, for her father was in the next room and the very first line of Aunt Isabel's letter had said:

1

"Keep this from your father."

"Haven't had time to read more than the first page," answered Carol, in a low voice. She was carefully putting the shirts into a sort of tray in the big suitcase. "But she's coming here as soon as Dad gets away, she says."

"How did she know he was going? We hardly knew it ourselves a week ago—that he was to be a delegate to the convention. How did Aunt Isabel find out—so far away and she hardly ever writes to us." Cecy was, as usual, very curious.

"From the glimpse of the letter I had," went on Carol, indicating that she had hidden the missive in her blouse, "Aunt Isabel read in the paper that Dad was to go to Chicago. Then she made up her mind."

"To what?" Cecy almost spoke aloud and glanced apprehensively at the door of the room where her father was going over his papers for the last time.

"To come to see us," said Carol. "She's going to explain."

"But why wait until Dad is away? He and she are great friends. I can't understand."

"Neither can I, Cecy. But it must be for some good reason. Now hurry! Tie those tags on the two bags. That's part of this job of helping pack and we undertook to do it."

"Yes, I know," Cecy wrinkled her nose in a puzzled way. "But why Aunt Isabel—and so all of a sudden? Didn't she even hint at something in her letter?"

Carol shot a look at the door of the next room. Then, bending closer to her sister she said, in a whisper:

"Yes, she did. It has something to do with Rocky Cliff."

"That old ancestral hall of hers out on the sea-coast where the stormy winds do blow, do blow, do blow?" Cecy was getting more excited.

"The very place," answered Carol. "Only Aunt Isabel says she is thinking of changing the name to Moaning Cliff."

"Moaning Cliff!" Cecy was clearly startled. "Whyever for?"

"Because of something that has happened or is happening there in the old mansion. She did no more than hint, on the first page of her letter—all I had time to read before Dad saw me and I remembered what Aunt Isabel said—not to let him know. So I hid it. So we must wait until he gets away."

"I can hardly wait."

"We must. It won't be long now. Dad goes on the 11:45 and Aunt Isabel arrives on the 12:07."

"Pretty close connections," remarked Cecy. "Did she give you the time of her train in the letter?"

"Naturally."

"But she didn't say why Rocky Cliff is to be changed to Moaning Cliff?"

"I don't know that it is—she just hinted at that, as she insinuated that something strange was going on at the queer old place and I imagine she's afraid it is something more serious than just stories."

"Afraid! Aunt Isabel?"

"I gathered that from her letter."

"And you only glanced at the front page!" mocked Cecy. "What will it be when you read the whole document?"

"I wish I knew," admitted the other girl. "But it looks as if we might be in for it again."

"You mean another Melody Lane mystery?"

"Rocky Cliff is a long way from Melody Lane," said Carol, dreamily.

"Yes, but if we go there a good part of Melody Lane will go with us," spoke Cecy, half laughing. "Oh, I do wish——"

"How you coming on, girls?" broke in the voice of Mr. Duncan.

"All finished, Dad," answered Carol.

"The last bag is packed and locked." This from Cecy.

"Well, that's just fine!" he greeted his daughters as he came from the other room. "I didn't think you could manage so well on short notice. Who would be bothered with a boy around when girls can be so efficient?" and there was pride in his voice and a smile in his eyes.

"I had no idea of going to this convention," he went on, "but I'm rather glad they sent me, as it's important. I shall enjoy it, though I shall miss my girls."

Carol's fingers rustled the letter hidden in her blouse. What else would her father miss besides his daughters if Aunt Isabel's hints materialized? Then she said:

"Your extra hankies are in the little pocket of this bag, Dad. They are for crying out loud at the business meetings when your motions are ignored by the chairman."

"Good!" he laughed.

"And your soft slippers are right on top, with your black pajamas in *this* bag," Cecy indicated. "They're for long rests on late mornings when it rains."

"Fine! Fine! But what about your long rests and late mornings? Are you girls going to have any fun while I'm away?"

"We'll try, Dad," said Cecy.

"The best we can," added her sister, her fingers again straying to the hidden letter. She was hoping her father's train would not be late and that Aunt Isabel's would be on time. She didn't want the two to meet. Felix Duncan would certainly think it very strange to see his aunt arriving with no previous word to him. The secret must be kept until the proper time for disclosure.

The bags were quickly tucked into the small

family car. Carol took the wheel and Cecy sat in the rear holding her father's hand. The faithful housekeeper, Rachel, waved a good-bye to Mr. Duncan from the front porch and called something about damp sheets. It made little impression, however.

The girls talked more excitedly during the ride to the station. They were keyed up about the strange letter and the impending visit. Then the last farewells and kisses were given, the last echoing rumble of the Chicago train died away. Dad was gone! The girls were to be alone with their housekeeper, Rachel.

In the short interval before the train arrived, Carol and her sister learned from reading the letter, that their father's rather aged and eccentric aunt was coming to them for help in a peculiar situation, having something to do with a terror or menace that seemed to surround her big estate—an estate that had come to her through inheritance, but where she had lived only for a short time, many years ago. Then she had decided it was too large for her simple tastes, though she declared the sea air of Rocky Cliff agreed with her as well as did some of the boasted climates of European springs. But she had put the place on the market for rent as, owing to a peculiar will, this must be done if she did not occupy it herself.

"She says," remarked Carol, as she passed the letter to her sister, "that unless some weird situation around the old mansion can be cleared up she is likely to lose the whole place."

"Yes, I read that," Cecy said, soberly.

"What can she mean, Cecy?" Carol was reasoning, rather than asking.

"Don't ask me. I thought there would be more to the letter. It was mostly all on the front page, after all, wasn't it?"

"Yes. But she will soon be with us, and then we'll know."

"Don't you feel a little guilty keeping it from Daddy?"

Carol hesitated a moment. Then she said: "No. It's Aunt Isabel's doing—not ours. She can explain to Dad."

"I suppose so. Well—here's the train!"

"I wonder if we'll recognize her when she gets off? She'll be in a Pullman, of course, and though we haven't seen her in a long time, she can't have changed much. People don't, at her age."

"Just what is the old age?"

"Oh, around seventy, I imagine," Carol replied.

"Then there she is, I guess!" The train had rumbled in and hissed to a stop. Cecy pointed to a dignified old lady who was alighting spryly from the Pullman coach, almost disdaining the well meant attentions of the porter with his rubber-topped step. The old lady came toward the girls at once, as Cecy jumped out and went to meet her.

"I couldn't mistake you, though you have grown

—lots!" the lady smiled. "You've grown prettier, too, if you don't mind me saying so," she was quick to remark.

"Not in the least!" laughed Cecy. "We only hope you mean it."

"And we knew you!" added Carol, pressing the outstretched hand affectionately.

"That's nice. I imagine it would be embarrassing to go up to a number of old ladies and try to get at me through the process of elimination," she laughed. "Well, I'm here!" she announced gaily, and there was a grim tightening of her lips and a defiant look in the eyes, bright in spite of her years. "Your father has gone, hasn't he?" She seemed anxious about this.

"Just got off before you arrived," said Cecy.

"But you didn't—didn't tell him?" she asked anxiously.

"Not a word—he didn't even see your letter," answered Carol.

"That's as I wanted it. What a nice little car you have!"

"It goes," Cecy said, assisting the visitor in and showing the porter where to put the bag. There was only one, the girls noticed, which indicated a brief visit.

"Now, Aunt Isabel," said Cecy when she was with the old lady on the back seat and Carol was again driving, "if you don't mind satisfying our terrible curiosity. I hate to rush you, but we're dying to hear the story."

"I know it must be irritating, girls, and I assure you I am going to startle you a little. But not another word until I have gotten into a kimono, and have had a cup of tea. I hope you have tea," she said. "I love a good cup of tea."

"You shall have the best cup of tea Rachel can brew," promised Cecy, "and she brags about *her* brand herself."

"Rachel?" There was a note of inquiry in the voice.

"Our housekeeper, you know."

"Oh, I'm glad you have one. She can go with you, I suppose, now that your father is away. I have forgotten how you run things."

"Rachel is to go with us—where, Aunt Isabel?" Carol flung back over her shoulder.

"That comes after the cup of tea," was the smiling reply. "So the sooner I have that——"

Carol's answer was to press down the accelerator, and the little car shot forward at a more rapid speed.

CHAPTER II

"WHY MOANING CLIFF?"

MELODY LANE was reached in rather less time than Carol and her sister usually made the trip from the station. Aunt Isabel now looked approvingly at the house and grounds.

"I haven't been here before," she observed.

"No," said Carol, "we weren't here when you visited us last."

"A lot has happened in Melody Lane since you were on to see Dad," remarked Cecy.

"Melody Lane," murmured the old lady. "I didn't know you called it that."

"How do you like it?" Cecy wanted to know.

"Charming—like yourselves. I left two little girls with Felix and come back to find two young ladies—a nice change. And now, my dears, I know you'll excuse me if I say I could do admirably with that cup of hot tea and a little rest. Then—well, you shall hear all about——"

"The mystery!" impulsively exclaimed Cecy and then, blushing, she drew back—they were all standing on the front porch. "I beg your pardon, Auntie," Cecy murmured humbly.

"Granted, my dear. No harm done. As a matter of fact it is a mystery."

Carol and Cecy looked at each other. Their aunt—great aunt to be exact—caught the exchange of glances.

"Don't you like mysteries?" she asked.

"Of course!" declared Carol.

"Only," stipulated Cecy with a little sigh, "if it's going to be one like the Wild Warning, which caused Carol so much———"

"It didn't cause me anything, my dear. Don't say that," objected Carol, a bit sharply. "I liked it."

"I don't see why girls shouldn't like mysteries and secrets," went on the old lady with a smile. "I did when I was your age. Gracious, yes! But things have changed a lot since those days! Oh, indeed yes!" and she laughed. "Now, if you don't mind, I'm going to have my tea and then I'll explain my letter and my visit which, I can guess, have mystified you, haven't they?"

"A little, yes, Aunt Isabel," admitted Carol. "And you shall have your tea at once."

"I don't want to be a bother, my dear, but, you see, I have health rules I must follow and one is that I mustn't get over-tired."

"It isn't wise," Carol gravely observed. It was rather difficult to carry on a conversation when, all the while, at the back of her head, Carol was wondering what it all would lead to.

Rachel was summoned and was presented to the visitor, and she promised to set the tea to brewing at once.

"Do you like it strong, Aunt Isabel?" Cecy asked.

"Not too strong, my dear. I must think of my nerves."

"And I'll show you to your room, if you are ready," said Carol.

"That's good of you. I'd like to let down a little."

"I think you are just splendid to travel alone and in summer time, too," Carol remarked, as she led the way to the green trimmed room they had prepared for Aunt Isabel.

"Well, you know, dear, mere infants are sent across the ocean alone these days," Miss Duncan replied, "and I can at least talk better than an infant, I hope."

"Well, my idea is," Carol said bravely, "that those mere infants, sent across the ocean with tags around their necks like poodles, are to be pitied. Why should those who are responsible for children try to put them off on those who have no reason to care for them?"

Aunt Isabel paused as she faced the door of her room. She put out her hand and impulsively clasped Carol's.

"Sensible, my dear. You are a thoroughbred Duncan."

When their aunt had been safely ensconced in her room, Carol and Cecy had a moment for a "breathing spell," in that fluttery morning.

Cecy had mentioned "The Wild Warning," which is the title of the book immediately preceding this in the Melody Lane mystery series. Carol and Cecy were the daughters of Felix Duncan and both figured preëminently in the volumes "The Mystery of Melody Lane," "The Tower Secret," and "The Forbidden Trail." In fact, it seemed that all the mysteries of Melody Lane, that quaint little settlement, now almost a village, had been centered around Carol, Cecy and their young friends.

The Duncan girls lived with their widowed father, and Rachel, the efficient Scotch housekeeper, in a small town in an Eastern state. Mr. Duncan often said it seemed as if the village lived with his family, so often was the old picturesque house filled with gay and jolly boys and girls. Among them was Thalia Bond, an especial chum of Carol's, Rosalind Wells, Cecy's "twin" as was often remarked and Glenn Garrison, a good-looking young man, and a very special chum of Carol's. They had been friends from Grammar into High classes.

"Let's dress," suddenly proposed Cecy, when Rachel had told them that their aunt was resting comfortably in her room and had asked her to say that she would be down in a half an hour.

"Dress!" exclaimed Carol. "What do you mean?"

"I mean let's put on something nice. I feel so frowsy after all that packing and hurrying this morning. I'm going to sponge off and put on my burnt orange. It makes me look so rugged."

"Then I'll wear my light green," decided Carol. "It makes me look so—refined!" and she laughed a little. Carol was dark and handsome; Cecy was blonde, and pretty in a dainty way in spite of her "cat's eyes" as she called them, and her mousey hair, also her own idea.

The girls were now freshly attired and sitting in the cool living room which was in welcome contrast to the outside heat of the early July day, waiting for Aunt Isabel to come down. They could hear her moving about upstairs. They really knew very little about her. She was more than a relative of their father's—she was something of a tradition in the Duncan history—reputed to be wealthy, if not rich, of a strange, domineering character at times, and again most friendly and gracious. She had always remembered the girls' birthdays with simple but welcome gifts.

"I do wish she'd hurry!" murmured Cecy getting up to pace the room.

"Don't show your impatience," warned Carol. "She may be the kind that turns contrary, like a balky horse, and if she sees we're eager she may keep us on edge. I suppose her visit and the letter both have something to do with Rocky Cliff—or Moaning Cliff. What a weird name!"

"It does sound spooky," admitted Cecy. "And I tell you right now, you nor Aunt Isabel can't get me to go out there. It's too far for one thing. Why should we go, anyhow? I'm so fed up with ghosts around here that I can hear my own bones rattle."

"Don't worry," retorted her sister. "I don't love spooks myself. We have always declared there are none, that we're not in the least bit afraid, and all that stuff. Then we get right into the mix-ups and change our minds. But here comes Aunt Isabel. Now for the fireworks!"

Isabel Duncan came slowly down the stairs, looking much refreshed and rested. She had been traveling over night and part of the day, but the short rest had done wonders for her. She really was a striking appearing woman, and in spite of her obvious seventy years, was more sprightly than many a younger person.

"I suppose you have been wondering why I wrote as I did and why I came on, waiting until I knew your father would be out of the way, my dears?" began Aunt Isabel, as she settled gracefully into the rocker Cecy pulled forward for her.

"There is no use denying that we are——"

"Just dying with curiosity!" broke in Cecy.

"Don't blame you a bit. Well, now for it—at least as much of it as I know." She smoothed out her soft silk dress and continued:

"You know, it has to do with the old inheritance

of mine. I won't go into the story of how the place was left to me by my grandfather, or try to untangle the snarled branches of the Duncan family tree. It has nothing to do with this matter. Enough to say, that the will is a novelty. Under it, in order to legally claim possession of Rocky Cliff, I must either live on the place myself, or make some profitable use of it—such as renting it and taking the money—which I don't really need as I have enough to last me while I live—an annuity and all that." She waved her white hand to dismiss such an unpleasant topic. "But still, I don't want to lose that place," she concluded wistfully.

"I don't blame you," agreed Carol.

"I don't remember much about it," added Cecy. "We were only there once when we were tiny tots."

"I remember your visit with pleasure, my dears. It seems a long time ago but it really wasn't. Now let me ask *you* something."

Aunt Isabel gave a quick, furtive look over her right shoulder and then one over her left. She was sitting with her back to a wall without windows, but Carol and Cecy could not help thinking that the old lady acted as if she thought some one might suddenly appear behind her, which idea was absurd, of course.

Then she glanced toward the door into the hall and murmured: "Will you please close that?"

"Why, Aunt Isabel!" objected Carol. "Won't you be too warm?"

"I don't mind if I am. I don't want any but you girls to hear what I am going to say."

"There is no one here but Rachel," Carol reminded her.

"Well, she's the one I don't want to hear, especially if she is going to Rocky Cliff with you."

"Are you sure *we* are going?" asked Cecy with a wink at her sister.

"I hope you will do me that favor, my dears," said the old lady who had lost her rather domineering air and was plainly beseeching. "That's what I came all the way from Hansonville to ask you. Please don't refuse me."

"We'll do anything we can for you—Dad would want us to," said Carol. "But perhaps it would be better to wait until he comes back——"

"No, no, my dear! He must know nothing of this. It isn't that I want to deceive him, but I know Felix Duncan better than you do. He would be sure to dissuade me—tell me to stop fighting fate. But I feel I must. Something seems to drive me on!" Her quick breath betrayed her feelings, and there was now an excited but purposeful look in the eyes of Aunt Isabel. Carol determined to help such a brave fight; but Cecy only became more suspicious.

"Now I must get along with my story," the aunt said next. "Can you two recall the visit you paid to me at Rocky Cliff?" She looked from one to the other awaiting an answer.

"Vaguely," said Cecy. "It seemed like a lovely old house and wonderful grounds, as I remember. Then, too, the view from the great cliff which the waves of the ocean bay break against—I remember hearing the great splash."

"I see you have a good picture of my old place," interrupted the aunt, "although you were very young when you visited there. How about you, Carol?"

"Well, I remember all that," said the older girl, slowly "but I also seem to remember that there was a certain gloom about Rocky Cliff. We were always listening for something."

"My dear, you have hit it exactly!" broke in her great-aunt. "Gloom! That's the word! The longer I lived there the more I found it piling up on me like a mountain, until at last, I could stand it no longer. And now, the gloom—well, I mustn't lay it on too thick," and she laughed a little at the trite expression. "But something must be done. There is some secret or mystery to be discovered at Rocky Cliff and I think you girls are brave and clever enough to solve it. Men are so terribly wise," she scoffed, "they just poo-poo the whole thing. Never admit it is there—but it is."

"Are you coming with us—if we go?" asked Cecy.

"Oh, no, my dear! It would never do. I may have been the cause of the—well, I won't name them. But I want something cleared up and I am depending on you. Your father wrote me about some of the things you had done here in Melody Lane in the way of investigating, and that gave me my cue."

"Oh, it was all very simple," said Carol smilingly. "Mysteries can be solved if we only go at them well—reasonably."

"It was almost silly at times," laughed Cecy. "So simple that every one overlooked the answers."

"Still, at times it must have appeared dangerous, didn't it?" asked the old lady critically.

"Yes," admitted Carol, slowly, "it did. But at Moaning Cliff——"

"That's only my nickname for it," her great-aunt made haste to say. "I dare say, it was all imagination. But here is the story.

"My grandfather was a miller from Holland, as was his father before him. Our family history has a legend to the effect that in the early Colonial days of our country my great-grandfather was virtually kidnapped aboard a ship and brought to this country because competent millers were very scarce and much needed by the colonists. However that may be, there has always been a mill in our family up to within recent years."

"Why, I remember a mill at Rocky Cliff!" exclaimed Carol.

"Yes, my dear, there is a small one there. It doesn't operate any more, but did in my grandfather's day. The farmers used to bring their grist to him to be ground. The great water wheel is there and the grinding stones, the upper and nether, but they don't turn now. The old wheel is covered with moss. The flume is, I suppose, dangerously slippery with green slime, and the mill pond must be almost hidden behind the rushes and cat-tails. But the mill building is there."

"What's the flume?" asked Cecy.

"Oh, that's the wooden trench that leads the water from the pond over the wheel to turn it."

Cecy nodded understandingly and Aunt Isabel resumed:

"Once I thought of putting the mill in order but I was told it would cost too much. For that matter, I have already spent on the old house and grounds more than I'll ever get out of it, even if I can keep the place. You'll see when you get there. Yes, there is a mill," her voice seemed to trail off dreamily and she seemed to be living in the past. "There is also a gate-house at the big entrance—the caretaker's, an elderly couple—live there now—if they haven't already been frightened away."

"Frightened!" gasped Cecy.

"Yes," her aunt nodded. "I may as well be frank with you," she went on. "There is some sort of terror at Moaning Cliff." Once more she glanced nervously over her shoulder and, almost imperceptibly, drew her chair closer to those of the girls.

"Why Moaning Cliff?" asked Carol determinedly.

"I don't really know," her aunt admitted. "Call it a whimsy of mine, if you will. Though," she went on in a voice the girls scarcely could hear, "Jensen did mention moans. But I didn't believe him. Now, my dears, here is the whole story in a little nutshell," she concluded more brightly.

"As I told you, I have tried to rent the place, but none of the tenants will stay more than a few weeks. I tried letting it to a man and wife who wanted it for tourists. They moved out quick enough. Next, I had a doctor in it. He thought it would be fine for a sanatorium, but after a few weeks he wrote me that he never could keep a patient there. They wouldn't stay. Nobody will stay, and I am likely to lose my inheritance because I can't live there myself nor let it for profit."

"Why won't they stay?" asked Carol. It seemed now that the aunt had obtained their promise to go to Rocky Cliff, she was giving some secrets away.

"Frankly, girls, I don't know. And I don't want to deceive you, either." Again that quick, furtive glance behind her. "There is something wrong, I am sure of that, for all these people who have tried to live there couldn't be deceived about such things, and I've had enough folks there to believe at least some of the stories. So you see, I had a very special reason in wanting to come to see you, to talk over things I couldn't write about and at a time when your father would be away so he could not spoil my little plans."

A serious look came into her eyes. . . . Carol thought it was a look much like her father's when his brown eyes pondered deeply.

"It is now or never, girls," said their aunt. "Will you try it?"

"You mean, we are to go out to your big house and live there?" asked Carol.

"Yes, my dear. Stay there long enough to find out it and then report to me. I'll finance the whole thing. You can have all the company you want. You know it's a wonderful place—acres of it!"

"Oh! Let's go, Carol!" suddenly proposed Cecy. "Let's go and take a crowd and Rachel. Some of the boys can come over from camp—Glenn isn't far from there, is he? And— Oh. Let's go!" She jumped up and clapped her hands, for when Cecy wanted adventure or fun she went right after it.

"That's the kind of a girl I thought I'd find," applauded Aunt Isabel in apparent relief. "I thought I could count on the daughters of Felix Duncan. What about you, Carol?"

"Oh, of course I'll go. In fact, I think it will be quite wonderful. This summer has been all broken up in little pieces anyhow, and maybe your plan, Aunt Isabel, will salvage the wreck for us."

"If I knew of or even imagined there was any danger you may be sure I wouldn't suggest it," declared the old lady vigorously as if trying to convince herself on that score. "And I'm no simple old soul, either. I go places and I see things. But out at Rocky Cliff——" she did not finish the sentence, but got up from her chair and, striding across the room, quickly opened the door Carol had closed at her request. When she found the hall vacant she gave a palpable sigh of relief. She smiled to explain her nervousness and then said: "Well, if you are to go, there is no time to lose. Summer ends as suddenly as it begins and I want to get this business settled and go to Georgia for my warm springs cure."

"Are you ill, Aunt?" asked Carol.

"No, not exactly, just trying to cheat the years." She laughed. "It can be done—up to a certain point. Now, it's decided—you'll go?" She seemed to wait eagerly, anxiously for their answers.

"Yes," said Cecy impulsively.

"Yes," echoed Carol. "But the preparations——"

"I'll take care of them. I'll telegraph the caretakers, Emil Jensen and his wife Mona, and let them know you are coming. You won't have to take a thing but your clothes. The place is fully furnished and I have ordered that it be kept aired. Your food you can buy in the little fishing village at the foot of the great cliff. I'll pay for everything, of course, even to your railroad fares. Now I'll go prepare the telegram. I can't tell you how much I appreciate this."

She hurried from the room just as footsteps were heard on the front porch. Cecy rushed to the long, low window to look out and see who was coming just as Carol murmured:

"But she didn't tell us yet why she called it Moaning Cliff?"

CHAPTER III

"LOOK! LOOK!"

"LOOK! Look!" exclaimed Carol, pointing with dramatic suddenness.

"We are looking," returned Thalia Bond. "It's terrible enough without you acting so about it!"

"But what is it?" asked Cecy. "It looks like a man masquerading——"

"The skeleton in armor!" murmured Carol. "Only I hope there is no skeleton in it."

"But what a horrible, grinning face!" whispered Thally.

"The better to scare you, my dear!" mocked Cecy.

Then, the first edge having been taken off their fright, for it had been a fright when they first entered the hall of the old mansion, called, so many years, Rocky Cliff, but renamed, by Aunt Isabel Duncan as Moaning Cliff, the three girls approached closer to the strange object standing in the dim darkness at the end of the long, dark corridor.

"Maybe he does the moaning," suggested Thally with a nervous little laugh.

"We'll soon see!" declared Carol boldly as she strode vigorously toward the horrible figure—for it was horrible, especially the face or, rather, the place where a face would have appeared had there been a man within the antique suit of Chinese armor. But in place of a face was a wooden mask, painted in reds and blues, with terrorizing, death-white lines streaked about the cruel, grinning mouth. Long hair, seemingly from the tail of a horse, hung down on each side of that leering, evil mask-face.

"Carol—be careful!" Cecy breathed a warning. "Those things spring right out and gobble you up."

"Yes, do!" urged Thally. "Where is Rachel?"

"Don't bring her in yet—until I have investigated," Carol ordered. "That is, if we want her to stay with us."

"And we surely do," declared Cecy. "I wish we had Glenn, and Bob and a few more of the boys if this is a sample of what we are going to run against in Rocky Cliff. Ugh! It's too awful!"

By this time Carol, acting more bravely than she really felt, for she was, actually, "showing off" a bit before her chums, had reached the side of the suit of armor and, by an investigating hand discovered that it was untenanted and seemed harmless.

"Aunt Isabel never warned us we should find this here," complained Cecy.

"Before we get through spending this vacation," suggested Thally as she kept at a respectful distance from the figure, "we may find that your aunt left out a lot of things she might have told us about."

"We mustn't think that Aunt Isabel deliberately deceived us," said Carol. "She wouldn't do that for the world and she assured me there was really nothing here to harm us—just something mysterious that needs discovering. That's why we're here. If she had thought about this Chinese warrior she would have mentioned it, because she remarked about our getting here when it would be almost dark. But there was so much excitement— she was hurrying back home so she could start her annual water cure, we were hurrying and packing to come here—there was so much to do, I suppose Aunt Isabel never thought of this." She waved a slim white hand toward the grinning figure.

"I never heard of the old thing. Maybe it clatters its bones and makes all the trouble. I don't believe it was here when we visited here the last time," declared Cecy.

"That was years ago, child," said Carol. "Aunt Isabel or some of her quick-moving tenants may easily have acquired the thing since and left it here when they hurried out." She was actually touching the metallic-clawed hands.

"Why were the tenants always moving out and

in such a hurry?" asked Thally. She had been told that much, and she too was now poking a finger at the old giant.

"That's what we're here to find out," suggested Cecy. "I think Aunt Isabel has sort of made us the 'goats' for this silly job."

"Nonsense!" declared Carol. "There must be something strange about this old place," she admitted, looking up into the dimness of the stairway where another long hall gave access to various bedrooms, "but this Chinese giant has nothing to do with it. He's just ornamental," and she picked up the gauntleted left hand (the other supported a long lance) and let it fall with a clang against the armor-plated thigh.

Cecy jumped back and the girls laughed at her.

"If he is ornamental then I'm a beauty cream!" declared Thally.

By this time all three girls had gathered enough collective courage to carefully inspect the armored figure in the dim light of the summer evening. It stood on a wooden pedestal, which added to the height, though it was tall enough without that. It was a complete suit of ancient and rare Chinese armor hung upon a frame, as are the suits of English mail armor in museums. Thus was given the effect of a man inside the bronze plates. For Chinese armor, unlike that of the English knights, was made of thin overlapping plates of a metal resembling bronze. It did not seem as heavy as

English armor about which our girls had studied
in English Lit. but perhaps was quite as effective.
It was also more ornamented than the trappings of
Richard of the Lion Heart, with dangling stream-
ers of horses' hair and gay pieces of cloth. The
most striking part was the face, or the mask that
had covered the face. It was the face of a grinning evil spirit.

"The Chinese believed," said Carol, in rather a
dreamy sort of voice, "that it was better policy to
scare your enemy to death than to actually kill
him. That's why the ancient warriors wore these
terrible masks."

"Let's turn it to face the wall," suggested Thally,
"I can't bear to have it staring at me. I'm afraid
he'll wink."

"We'll get used to it in time, I suppose," remarked Cecy. "Besides, it doesn't seem easy to
move—rather heavy," and she put a foot against
the pedestal on which the armored figure stood and
shoved. It did not move an inch.

"Let it alone," advised Carol. "When some of
the boys come over we'll get them to shift it—that
is, if it still annoys us."

"It would always annoy me," said Thally with
a slight shiver. And this was Thally-the-brave,
afraid of an old armor.

"You speak of the boys coming over," suggested
Cecy, with a questioning look at her sister.

"Yes. You know Glenn is swimming instructor

at Tagawah Camp only a few miles from here and
Ted Morton, a new friend of Glenn's, has charge
of teaching the young boys how to handle boats.
Glenn said they would be over to see us sooner or
later. And now," went on Carol, "it's about time
we started getting to rights if we are going to
make Rocky Cliff our summer headquarters and
help Aunt Isabel retain possession of her inheritance." A comic sigh that ended in a groan punc-
tuated that.

"If it was mine," murmured Thally, "I'd give
the whole dump away and that old imp of Chinese
blackness with it," and she gave a wild look at the
grinning armored figure.

"Here comes Rachel," announced Cecy in a low
voice.

The housekeeper, who had come to Rocky Cliff
with the girls had been attending to their bags,
while the girls started their exploring. Rachel
wanted to pay the expressman who had brought
the baggage up from the railroad station. This
had now been done and she was on her way to
rejoin the girls. To their surprise she showed no
sign of alarm on beholding the figure in armor—
the evil sight of which had caused the girls some
excitement.

"Huh!" she murmured with an audible sniff.
"Another one of those horrible things!"

"What do you mean—another?" asked Carol.

"Oh, I used to work in a gentleman's house that

was full of them, and battle axes and spears and what-not. Nasty dust-catchers, if you ask me. And now, if you'll show me who is going to have which rooms, I'll get the beds made and see about supper. The stuff came from the grocery and he brought a piece of ice until we can get the electric refrigerator started."

"Oh, we're going to have all the comforts of home!" exclaimed Thally in delight. She loved her comforts, did Thalia Bond.

"Yes, Aunt Isabel had the place put in order for us," replied Carol. "It's queer Jensen and his wife haven't been in yet."

"Who is Jensen?" asked Thally.

"The caretaker; Emil Jensen. He and his wife live in a sort of lodge at the main entrance gate," Carol explained. "We came in the side gate. I suppose they don't know we have arrived, though Aunt Isabel wrote to them, she said. But now about beds."

"And eats!" added Cecy.

With Rachel, they went upstairs and were delighted to find the old mansion in much better order and showing more care than they had dared to hope for. The bedrooms were fresh and clean and the beds needed but the addition of linen and blankets to be completely ready.

Following Aunt Isabel's explanation of why she wanted Carol and Cecy to go to occupy Moaning Cliff, as she called it, an explanation given shortly after her arrival at their home and the consumption of various cups of tea, Thally had unexpectedly called at the Duncan home. Of course, Thally had to be told of the impending mystery, and of course she was invited to be of the investigating party.

"As if I wouldn't come!" she had exclaimed. "You couldn't lose me."

It was then that things had happened rapidly. Aunt Isabel, after sending word to the Jensen caretakers that her nieces were to live in Rocky Cliff that summer, had promptly departed for her own home several hundred miles from Melody Lane. From there she was to go to a warm spring health resort.

"Be sure to write me what happens," she charged Carol, "and stick it out if you can. Find what is driving all my tenants from the old house. I want to keep it for myself. I may want to make it my last home—after the water cure!" and she had laughed a laugh that was younger than her years.

So the girls had promised. They had rushed their preparations to get ready to come to Cedarshore, the name of the village on the great cliff on which was perched the old mansion that had descended in such a strange and cumbered inheritance to Aunt Isabel.

They had just now arrived, after a short stop in the little village to purchase supplies, and had entered the big estate by a side gate which, the driver of the rattling hack auto, had told them was a short cut. They found the house open and aired and then had come the discovery of the armored figure in the lower front hall.

"Well," remarked Carol when they had finished a casual inspection of the upper floor of the big house, "I don't see anything very terrible here."

"I did!" suddenly announced Thally.

"You did?" gasped Cecy. "Where?"

"When I looked in the glass. I'm a sight! So are you—and you!" She pointed an accusing finger at Carol and her sister.

"Oh, we must sponge off and get into some other clothes, even if it's only to satisfy our own pride," Carol declared. "Let's do some unpacking and then we'll have a bit of a wash."

Bedrooms were selected, each girl to have one to herself, but they were all in close proximity along the big hall. Meanwhile Rachel had gone down stairs and soon there began floating up aromas that told of an impending meal.

"And am I hungry!" exclaimed Thally as she began to change her dress.

"And am I warm!" murmured Cecy as, half undressed, she hurried to the bath room for a sponge.

"It's a lovely place, though, isn't it, in spite of the grim shadow that Aunt Isabel seemed to think is hanging over it?" asked Carol, as she stood at a window and gazed toward the picturesque mill outlined in dim shadows now. "I'm sure we shall love it here."

"If we don't get scared away by whatever your aunt said scared her tenants," said Thally. "How can *we* expect to escape?"

"Perhaps it was all imagination!" called Cecy between water splashings.

"Well, it isn't any imagination that we are going to have visitors!" suddenly announced Carol who had descended to the first landing of the stairway where a window gave a view across the fields.

"Who?" asked Thally.

"I'm not sure, but I think it's the caretaker, Jensen and his wife headed this way. Hurry, girls, and come down with me."

CHAPTER IV

THE FIRST NIGHT

EMIL JENSEN, the caretaker, was pleasant of face and manner yet sufficiently respectful to show, at first glance, that he was a caretaker. He had the estate-retainer appearance and his little wife, who patted along back of him, seemed anxious to please. Carol, Cecy and Thally had hurried their dressing and were ready to receive their visitors who were ushered into the dining room by Rachel. Appropriately enough, the Jensens had arrived by way of the kitchen where the housekeeper was preparing the meal.

"I guess you're the girls Miss Duncan wrote about, eh?" questioned Jensen as he nodded, and smiled while his wife, behind him, bowed rather more formally.

"Yes," admitted Carol. "Aunt Isabel said she would write to you about us. Won't you sit down?" She indicated chairs.

"No, thank you, miss. We just come up to see if everything was all right and if you had what you wanted. First time you come to a strange place there's generally something needed, and more the longer you stay."

35

"We intend to stay," said Cecy, a bit defiantly.

"Yes?" Jensen's voice was questioning.

"Why shouldn't we?" demanded Carol.

He shrugged his shoulders, looked out into the big hall where the shell of the Chinese warrior stood and replied:

"Well, most folks don't, or hasn't."

"Now, Emil," began his wife, "don't begin scaring the young ladies their first night here."

"Who's scaring 'em?"

"You're trying to, ain't you?" she scolded.

"Not a bit of it!" His voice was truculent—defiant. "I just answered her question. Maybe nothing won't happen at all." But his remark contradicted him.

"What has happened here?" Carol sharply inquired.

"I don't know," he did not meet her eyes. "Nothing ever happened to me or my wife—not a thing. But then," he added, before anyone could answer, "you see, we never spent a night here. I wouldn't—not of late years. No, sir!"

"You have said so much—you are bound to tell us more," declared Cecy. "Go on! At least tell us what you *do* know."

"I got nothing more to go on about," was the somewhat sullen answer. "Told you nothing ever happened to me or mine here. I'm not to blame for what folks say—am I?" He appeared hurt, as if he felt he needed to defend himself.

"No," Carol admitted, "but if you know of anything really important about this old house—something that causes those who have lived here to flee in terror—why don't you admit it—tell us so we can be on the lookout? *We* surely should know if anyone does."

"If I knew anything I'd tell you—honest I would," said Jensen, and he seemed sincere. "But all I know is, what those who lived here sort of half told me, when they come to give up the keys. And they never said anything you could put a finger on, so to speak. It was just that they didn't like the place and was going to move. It wasn't a question of breaking a lease for none of 'em ever signed one. Wait a bit, I'm wrong there, the first tenant I remember since your aunt, Miss Duncan owned the place, did have it on a lease. A doctor he was, and a queer chap. He had a lease and he started to make the place a sort of rest cure or sanitarium. Had some patients. But two of 'em died, the rest, that was able to get away, did get out, and your aunt wouldn't hold him to the lease after he said he couldn't keep the place going."

"You mean Miss Duncan canceled the lease?" asked Carol.

"If that's what you call it—yes. She is a nice person to deal with," he inserted. "After that, your aunt always said whenever anybody wanted to rent the place, that they should try it for a few months and then, if they wanted to stay, they could sign the papers, she was that generous. But none of 'em ever did."

"You mean they all ran away?" asked Thally, her eyes growing wider open as the grim tale proceeded. If everybody left how could these girls stay?

"Well, some walked," admitted the caretaker with an attempted joke. "But it come to the same thing in the end. They left. Now if you girls——"

"But what made them leave?" insisted Carol.

He twirled his cap. "That I can't say. All I ever heard from any of 'em was they couldn't stand the noises."

"Did they say *moaning?*" asked Cecy, glancing at her sister and Thally.

"Well, yes, I guess one or two did," admitted Mr. Jensen with hesitation.

"But they never *saw* anything!" his wife hastened to add. She seemed fearful that her husband would spoil things.

"No, none of 'em told me they ever *saw* anything," said the man. "So maybe you won't, and maybe you won't even hear anything. I hope you don't. But what I come for was to see if everything is all right." The tortured cap was finally straightened out properly.

"Everything is—*so far,*" said Carol, the emphasis being decided.

"I'm glad of that. I turned the water on, and

had the gas and electricity turned on soon as Miss Duncan wrote me you was coming. And I see you got in some supplies." He sniffed in the direction of the kitchen.

"Yes," said Carol. "I think we shall make out all right. But you will be available if we need— need help?" she asked half jokingly.

"Help?" He seemed a bit frightened at the idea.

"I mean if—anything happens."

"Oh—yes, of course. But maybe nothing will. I hope not."

"If we hear noises—moans—" Carol paused. That was rather a strong suggestion.

"Oh, you probably won't hear 'em," said Mrs. Jensen, comfortingly. "I don't believe half the folks that moved out heard anything more than the wind or the sea—you can hear that plain when the wind is right. And maybe," she added with a half smile, "some of 'em had bad dreams—nightmares."

"That's it!" hastily added Emil, too glad to agree.

"I don't believe any of us are subject to nightmares," said Cecy with a laugh—the first real laugh the girls had heard since coming to Rocky Cliff.

"But I'd like to get one thing settled," insisted Carol. "If anything happens and we do hear strange noises—what shall we do? Can we count on you?" She looked directly at Mr. Jensen.

"Oh, yes, Miss Duncan! Sure! Come to me any time. In the middle of the night. If you bang on my door or throw a pebble up at my window— I'm a light sleeper—I'll hear you."

"Thanks," Carol murmured. "But I hope we shan't have to awaken you in the middle of the night."

"Not if we are aroused by hearing moans and have to leave our warm beds and tramp a quarter of a mile in the dark; not for me!" declared Thally. "I would rather put up with a lot of noise."

"Well, I'll do all I can," said the caretaker. "Now, if there isn't anything we can do at present, me and my wife, we'll go back."

"Thank you," Cecy murmured. It seemed good to have help within call.

"You are sure you have all you want—in the way of bed things and stuff to eat?" asked Mrs. Jensen kindly.

"Oh, yes—plenty, thank you," Carol answered. "It was good of you to come."

"We'd have been here quicker if we'd known you had arrived," stated Emil, with a little air, as if he had, somehow, failed in his duty. "But you didn't come in the main gate——"

"No," said Carol, "the taxi driver said the side gate was the shorter way."

"So 'tis! So 'tis. But I'd seen you if you'd come past my house. The only way I knew you was here, was when my wife, who was up on the hill, happened to see dresses fluttering around. Then we guessed you'd come, so we hurried up. You see, we do a bit of farming—I raise stuff, sell some of it, eat some of it and that, with free rent for our house, makes it so your aunt don't have to pay us any money for looking after her place," Emil explained. "It's a good arrangement for both of us, I guess."

"Seems so," Carol admitted. "Well, thank you, again, for coming over. But we have everything for the present. Shall we see you again?"

"I didn't count on coming over again tonight," was the answer. "But—if you want me——"

"I don't believe we shall unless——"

"We hear moans!" broke in Cecy.

"Or that thing comes to life!" added Thally, nodding toward the figure in armor.

Emil Jensen chuckled.

"That thing!" he chuckled. "Well, it might, at that. The doctor—him I was telling you about who had patients die here—he left that statue. He was quite a character."

"Who?" asked Carol.

"Oh, the doctor. Did you think I meant *him?*" and Emil pointed to the warrior's shell. "No, he never was alive. It's just a sort of affair to put on when you're fighting, the doctor told me. But if it was mine I'd toss it off the cliff into the bay— where it's deepest—being iron it'd sink—deep."

"Why?" asked Cecy innocently.

"Why, miss, iron always does sink."

"I know that. But why would you sink the old warrior's Sunday suit?"

"Oh—I don't know—just wouldn't have it around, that's all. It's sort of disturbing to have to look at."

"It is a devil—a devil!" said Mrs. Jensen in a low voice. "Come on, Emil!"

They turned to leave, with further offers of help, and they were soon on their way along the tree-bordered path that led from the rear of the old mansion to the more humble cottage.

"Shall I serve now, Miss Carol?" asked Rachel, looking in from the butler's pantry.

"Yes, do, please. And then we'll take a walk around the place before it gets too dark. I like to see the layout even at twilight."

"To make sure no one is likely to play tricks," added Cecy. "Eh, Thally?"

"Oh, I don't know!" Her voice showed distress. "I hope we did right by coming here."

"We promised to help Aunt Isabel and I'm going to!" declared Carol firmly. "The keeping of this place in her possession means a lot to her at her age. She'll need it before she dies. Now let's eat."

The meal provided a lively change as it proceeded. It was not long drawn out, as the girls were anxious to get outside before the impending night darkened Rocky Cliff. And dusk was in the

offing as they finished and went to the edge of the
cliff, to watch the gloaming light paint magic over
the sea and bay.

Somewhere in the distance a dog howled dis-
mally.

"Oh, that's awful!" murmured Thally with a
little shudder.

"Why?" asked Cecy.

"Oh, I don't know—I just don't like it—that's
all there is to it."

"We mustn't be silly," chided Carol. "After all,
though we came here for a vacation, we have made
a promise to Aunt Isabel. We must make Rachel
go to bed now. She is so tired and so good to
have stuck around with us all day. I'll go find
her," she went on as they reached the house.
"Otherwise she may be dabbling around in her
precious kitchen for an hour more. Back in a moment," and she left Cecy and Thally to their own
devices for a little while.

The devoted housekeeper was, as Carol sus-
pected, still fussing around, locking windows and
attending to her refrigerator. Carol insisted that
she stop and go right to bed.

"Have you a flashlight?" Carol asked.

"Oh, yes, Carol-love. I keep mine under my
pillow."

"A good idea," Carol assured her. "Sometimes
the electric current in the country places at the sea-
shore, goes off unexpectedly. I'll leave a low light

burning in the lower hall, though," she decided. "Rocky Cliff is so rambly we might get up for something and be lost."

"That's thoughtful of you, Carol-love. And now I believe I'm through," Rachel announced with a last look around her kitchen. "Go ahead, my dear, and I'll snap off the light."

If the girls were timid about retiring, nothing was said about it. Their rooms were close together on the front of the house. Rachel's apartment, near the second bath room, was at the far rear. Having seen the housekeeper enter her bedroom, Carol hurried back along the extensive hall to make sure Cecy and Thally had everything they might need before she went to her own room.

"All right?" she first questioned Cecy, looking in at her sister from around the half-opened door.

"Why not?" Cecy countered. "Though I feel like a dishrag—so damp and limp. This salty air takes the starch out of everything."

"Yes, it does, even one's hair," Carol laughed.

"As if I didn't know! Mine's ruined. And I have my flashlight so you needn't examine me on that subject!" Cecy chuckled.

"Hope you don't need it—I mean for any midnight alarm," said Carol with an air of easiness.

"Here's hoping with you." Cecy cocked her pretty thumb and aimed a stiff forefinger at her sister in imitation of a pistol, at the same time clicking her tongue.

"Now be good, dear," the older girl coaxed and she touched Cecy's cheek with a little kiss.

"I will if I can," Cecy promised. "But remember this is *your* mystery."

"I'm not likely to forget it," and Carol went out of the room smiling.

Next she entered Thally's room. "All right?" she asked like a matron in a girl's boarding school making sure her charges were safely tucked in. "All right, Thal?"

"Yes, my dear, but I'd sleep better if that grinning evil spirit was out of the lower hall. I don't know when a man made such a *strong* impression on me!" and Thally doubled up with laughter.

"You mean the Chinese warrior?"

"Yes. I can't forget that grinning mask of a face, and I usually like smiling faces."

"We'll try and move it when Glenn and Ted come over—in a few days," said Carol. "I don't want to give Jensen the satisfaction of knowing that it bothers us."

"No. Don't. I'll be glad to see Glenn. And when is Rosie coming?"

Rosalind Wells had been invited by telephone at the last minute to form one of the party at Rocky Cliff and had promised to join her chums.

"She'll be here next week," Carol said. "And now to bed!"

"But," persisted Thally, "I just want to ask——"

"Now, no more talk," Carol ordered. "We really have a job on our hands," she said in a low voice that would not reach the possible listening ears of Cecy, "and it's my idea we should start right in training."

"Like 'sojers,' my dear," teased Thally. "But don't make us wear khaki uniforms. I stick out in the worst places. Besides, my freckles hate khaki." Thally was in her orange pajamas and if she stuck out in awkward places they didn't show just then.

"You're a love, Thal, and, believe it or not, I wouldn't have come here if you hadn't volunteered," said Carol.

"Hurray!" hissed Thally although Carol was frantically motioning for silence, with Cecy in mind. But Thally seemed irrepressible. "Oh, I love a parade!" she attempted to hum, at the same time picking up her flashlight, switching it on and off and strutting around foolishly but surely with comical effect. She ended by throwing her arms around Carol who lost no time in wiggling loose and escaping lest Thally's urge toward "sojering" became more noisy.

Then Carol entered her own room with a last, lingering look up and down the long hall that was faintly illuminated by the light which came up the stairway.

"I hope we all sleep well," the girl mused, as she slipped out of the robe she was wearing, placed her slippers on the side of the bed nearest the door and tucked her flashlight beneath her pillow. Then, after a brief pause, she snapped off the wall switch and stretched in luxurious comfort between the clean sheets Rachel had put on so smoothly.

At last silence and sleep settled down over the old mansion and not even the spirit of the kidnapped miller nor the wraith of the warrior who had once fought in the strange armor seemed swirling abroad to disturb the peace of the night. Only the soft swish of water on the shore of the bay and the distant, outer booming of the more violent ocean waves made echoes around Moaning Cliff.

Carol was not sure she had been asleep, and if she had slumbered she did not know for how long, when she was suddenly aroused by a moan.

She sat up in bed, her heart pounding violently and her hand trembling as she thrust it beneath her pillow.

Her nerves calmed a little as her fingers touched the cool metal of the little electric torch and she listened intently. There was no mistake about it —there was a moan faintly echoing through the vastness of the weird old house.

"Oh," thought Carol, trying to still the panic within her, "it's come! But this is my job—my responsibility. I must shoulder it——"

She swung her legs softly over the side of the bed, shielded the flashlight lens in one hand to throw a minimum of illumination about the room, found her slippers and thrust her feet into them. Then she reached for her robe on a chair nearby, thrust the still glowing torch partly beneath her pillow to curtain it and put the robe on. Then with the flashlight fully glowing she walked softly across the room and as softly opened her door. She thrust her head out into the hall, noting that the lower light was still burning, and listened.

She did not hear the moan or groan again, but she was as sure now, when fully awake, as she had been at first when half asleep, that she had heard a strange sound. What was it?

She flashed her light in turn first toward the door of Cecy's room and then toward Thally's. Both were closed and there was no sign nor sound of movement within.

"Both sound asleep, thank goodness!" Carol whispered. "Now I must see about Rachel. She may be in a panic of fear."

Softly she padded, like some stalking animal, down the long hall to the housekeeper's door. No light seeped beneath it. Carol tapped, lightly.

"Come in!" The housekeeper's voice betrayed no fear. She did not even ask who it was, but she switched on her light immediately and the room was bright as Carol entered.

"What is it?" Rachel asked.

"I heard a noise," said Carol in a low voice. "At least I think I did—but I've been thinking and anticipating so much that perhaps——"

She paused and looked questioningly at the housekeeper, whose face seemed lined with anxious wrinkles.

"I heard it, too, Carol-love. At least I heard a noise. I'm not sure it was what you heard——"

"A sort of moan. But it wasn't loud, Rachel. And, after a second thought I thought perhaps it might be you."

"Me?"

"Yes. In a sort of nightmare, you know. You've worked so hard today, and up into the night, helping us settle. I know you must be tired and when one is tired and falls into an early sound slumber——"

"I know, yes, my dear. I might easily have had the nightmare and have moaned in my sleep," said Rachel quickly. "It is quite possible. Now I recall it, when I awoke my throat was very dry, as if I had been sleeping with my mouth open—you do that in nightmare, you know."

"So I have heard. Well, if it was you, Rachel——" Carol was a bit doubtful.

"I feel quite sure, now, that it was," the housekeeper hastened to say. "That explains it. I'm sorry I frightened you. Too bad!"

"Oh, I don't mind that—only——"

"And we'll say nothing to the others about it," Rachel went on attempting a smile. "Don't worry. It will be all right, Carol-love," and she took Carol's hand within her own as she sat on the edge of the bed. "You'll be all right now—when you go back to your room."

"Oh, yes, of course—" Carol's voice trailed off and she glanced out of the half opened door toward the dim hall.

"Carol-love!" said Rachel quickly, "why not spend the rest of the night here with me?"

"With you?" Carol looked down at the bed—it was not full size.

"There's a lovely little alcove room opening off this, with a bed in it all made up. I saw to that. Sleep there."

It was a temptation too great to be resisted. "But I might disturb you, Rachel."

"More likely I am to disturb you—with my nightmare," she laughed softly. "But I never have it the second time. Do stay."

Quite honestly Carol felt that she was doing the housekeeper as much of a favor as she was herself. But with her usual devotion to duty the girl murmured:

"If Cecy or Thally should awaken——"

"Then they didn't hear the noise—I mean me?" Rachel added the last quickly.

"They didn't seem to. Their doors were closed when I came out of my room."

"Then they're all right."

"I suppose so."

"Do stay, Carol-love!" Rachel took both her hands now and pressed them fondly.

"I will." Carol moved toward the little alcove, Rachel preceding her to throw back the covers in a motherly way.

"Now, we'll be all right," said the faithful housekeeper. "And remember—not a word of this to the others."

"No; not a word."

For a long time Carol lay awake, staring up straight into the blackness after Rachel had switched off her light. Then came the slow, regular breathing of the woman. Carol began counting the respirations but she never knew the total for, without realizing it she, too, had fallen asleep.

CHAPTER V

A WARNING

CAROL DUNCAN awakened with a start to find the morning sun joyously flooding her little alcove nest. With grateful surprise she realized that there had been no other disturbance this first night. She looked out into the main bedroom and saw that Rachel was gone. A faint sound from the kitchen below told that the housekeeper was about her breakfast duties. Carol felt sure Rachel would remember their pact of secrecy and say nothing to the others of what had happened in the night.

"Well, that's that," Carol mused, as she swung her feet over the side of her bed, found her slippers and gown and started for her morning bath. Half way down the hall she met Cecy bent on the same errand. Cecy's face was still rosy from healthful sleep.

"Why, Carol!" the younger girl exclaimed, "what were you doing in Rachel's room so early?"

"Oh, you know the captain must be sure all his soldiers are to be relied upon," Carol answered easily.

"But you never have to get Rachel up in the morning."

"I know. She is already up. Sleep well?"

"Never better!"

"Hear anything of Thally?"

"Not during the night. We both slept like the proverbial bricks. But she's up now, getting ready to sing in her bath and doing the daily dozen—you know they only allow a half dozen now under the code," and Cecy yawned impressively.

"No, I wasn't aware of that. But I'm glad everything was all right."

"Why shouldn't it be?"

"Oh, you know what Aunt Isabel said."

"I'm beginning to believe," laughed Cecy, "that a good deal of that was, as the boys say, 'bunk,' Carol, my sweet. Now, shall we toss for the bath?"

"No, go ahead. I can wait." Carol passed on and saw Thally coming from her room, as happy and rosy as was Cecy.

"So far so good!" vigorously declared Thally. "No boogie mans got my little friend?" and she made a playful pass at Carol's ribs.

"Not a single boogie. And the big, bad Chinese Dragon didn't gobble you up, did he, Thally?"

"Not a gobble. But I dreamed of him—the monster!"

"You'll get used to him—you may even come to love him. But, at the same time," added Carol,

"I think, if any of the boys drop over for a visit, we'll have them shove Mr. Warrior into the big closet I saw in the back hall."

"That's right, shut the big, bad mans up in dark!" Thally "baby-talked" this.

After breakfast Cecy gaily proposed that they go out and look around the place.

"We didn't half see it last night," she declared, "as it was getting dusk when we arrived."

"Yes, we must take a look around," agreed Carol. "Come on, Thal!"

They hurried out. Their daylight view of the place, where they had come on a double errand— to spend the vacation time and also to try to unravel the mystery, confirmed what they had seen the evening before. The big house, bequeathed to Aunt Isabel under rather strange conditions, was perched on a great cliff at the bottom of which the waters of the bay surged peacefully over white and yellow sands at times, and again beat against the foot of the cliff and its adjacent rocks.

Just south of the house, where the cliff was split in twain as if by a giant's axe, flowed a tidal stream, too large for a brook, too small for a river. Clam Creek it was called by the man who had brought up from the railroad station such baggage as the girls had not fetched with them in their trip from Melody Lane to Cedarshore.

"You kin tred out lots of clams in that crick if you're so minded," he had told them then.

"I don't believe I'll be so minded," Carol had gaily replied.

The other girls had agreed with her. Thally said:

"It's too mucky."

"'Tis mucky," agreed the man with a chuckle, "but clams live in muck. Ye got t' know how t' tred 'em out barefooted."

This talk was remembered by the girls as they now walked, in the bright sunshine to the edge of the cliff and looked down upon the sands and rocks, which the low tide waters of the bay were but gently kissing.

The cliff on which Aunt Isabel's house stood, dominated the curving bay shore and even seemed to cast its shadow upon the surging ocean farther out, with its tumbling billows of green and white. Back of the house stretched a long, rolling plateau, with fields and patches of woods intermingling. In the far distance gleamed the waters of a little pond or small lake, from this distance the girls could not determine which. The fields did not seem to have been tilled. Probably they had long lain fallow following the death of the old, kidnapped miller, the Duncan pioneer. The mill still remained, at a considerable distance from the house, but the great wheel, once turned by the waters of Clam Creek no longer turned. It stood there, stark and lone, a mere ghost of its former power.

"We must explore the mill some day," said

Carol, as she turned back to again look down the sloping side of the great cliff.

"We'll get Jensen to pilot us," suggested Cecy, as she pointed to the cottage of the caretakers near the back gate entrance to the grounds. There was no sign of either Jensen or his wife just then.

"I believe we could get down there," said Cecy, after they had admired the view for a time, had circled the old mansion without discovering anything more than the faded and weed-tangled natural beauties of the grounds and had come back to the top of the cliff.

"Down where?" asked Carol.

"To the bottom of the cliff." Cecy pointed. "There's a path—not easy but we can make it, I think. A little exercise will be good after breakfast. And I'd sort of like to paddle my feet in the water—where that little brook runs into the bay. Let's go down!"

"It sounds enticing!" agreed Thally always ready for a lark.

"I'll not be the one to hold back," joined in Carol.

Presently they were scrambling and climbing down the cliff, using jutting stones and stunted bushes for handholds. After the usual girlish squeals they were soon down on the sandy beach and taking little steps like silly dances. The tide was now coming in, and there was an inviting stretch of sand near the little stream which came through a cleft in the rocks from the direction of the old house.

"Here goes!" cried Cecy, sitting down and beginning to take off her shoes and socks. "I love the feel of wet sand between my toes!" she laughed. "It's so oozy."

"Let's all paddle!" Thally giggled.

"It certainly ought to be cooling," said Carol, "but look out for holes."

The three barefooted girls, holding their short skirts at safer distance, were walking through the little washing waves on the shore of the bay, toward the end where the creek entered.

"Oh, this is delicious!" murmured Cecy. "Wait until I get on that stretch of shimmering, wet sand and then——"

A voice suddenly hailed them—a man's voice. They turned to see running toward them a rough-clad figure—obviously a fisher or lobsterman. He shouted:

"Keep away! Keep away from them sands! Don't go near 'em! It's dangerous! Keep away!" came urgent shouts.

Frozen with sudden terror at the man's shouts Carol, Cecy and Thally stood with uplifted skirts, feeling the damp sands of the bay shore upon their bare feet and looking in wonder at the man who was now lumbering toward them. He ran as one does who is accustomed to stand with spread legs against the heave and fall of a sloping boat deck beneath him. As he came nearer, the girls looked at his tanned face—like the face of a rugged Norseman done in bronze, and saw beyond him where his boat was drawn upon the beach near, a pile of tarred lobster pots.

"Keep away from them sands!" he called again, almost shaking his fist at them.

"Why?" asked Carol, for now they could talk without shouting as he was almost beside them as they stepped on the safer shore.

"Quicksands, that's why! You're likely to sink down in 'em. The tide's just right now—they're bad—keep away from 'em," he ordered excitedly. "It's a wonder the folks you're stopping with didn't warn you about 'em."

"We aren't stopping with anyone—we're here by ourselves," said Carol. "But I suppose some one around might have warned us."

"They sure ought to," declared the lobsterman. "Foolish not to. An' if anybody asks you who said so tell 'em Jed Bailey—that's my name. Folks buys lobsters off me around here. Maybe you might want some. Where you stoppin' at?"

Carol pointed in the direction of the big house atop the mass of stone, that seemed to hold the gentle bay and the more turbulent ocean from encroaching on the land.

"Oh, up at Moaning Cliff!" His manner underwent a sudden change. He seemed to draw into his shell and he had a suspicious air about him, sort of skeptical. "So you're stopping there."

"We have come there to live," said Cecy, with assumed indifference.

"Live there?" he exclaimed in surprise.

"Just for the summer," Carol hastened to say. "It's my aunt's place—Miss Isabel Duncan."

"Oh, yes. I know her. She used to live here. Used to buy my lobsters too. But of late I haven't sold any up at Moaning Cliff." He shook his head ruefully.

"Will you tell me something?" Carol suddenly asked, smiling with real friendliness at the weather-beaten fisherman.

"Why, yes. Sure! You mean them sands I warned you about?" He pointed to a yellowish stretch that was now being invaded by the tide, slowly but surely.

"About them—yes," said Carol. "But also why do they call my aunt's place Moaning Cliff?" The question was sudden. The reaction of Jed Bailey, the lobsterman, was just as sudden. He shot quick glances from one girl to the other and countered warily:

"Didn't she tell you?"

"She started to," Carol was quick to say, "but we came away in a hurry and she didn't have time. Perhaps you can explain."

As the three waited anxiously—even apprehensively—the lobsterman answered, with a shake of his head:

"No," he stated, "I can't. Not but what I would if I could. But all I know is that folks who live in there—I mean since your aunt moved away—talk about queer noises—like mo-an-s." He drew the last word out till it moaned itself. "But what makes 'em I don't know. And if people who was in there knew they never told. But about these sands—I can tell you about *them* and then maybe you'll keep away from 'em, when you understand."

"We surely will if they're dangerous," Thally assured him.

"Well, they are—I'm telling you. They're quicksands. If you don't know what that means. It's that you'll sink quick in 'em. You see, ordinary sand, when it's wet, packs hard and you can walk on it, whether or not it's covered with water. But quicksand is different. I've read that the grains are so round, instead of being sharp and pointed, that they keep rolling and turning over and over, quick like. Well, whatever it is, we got quicksands here," he declared emphatically. "They ain't no bottom to 'em, seems like. You can walk out at the sea beach or at the bay beach, most places, and your feet sink down in the sand a little ways and then you strike rock or clay bottom and that's all there is to it.

"But these sands, here at Clam Creek—they're **treacherous**," he went on, "like a sting ray who

gets you in the foot with the horn on the end of
his tail," he said, explaining the antics of that queer
fish with the swordlike tail. "You walk out there,"
and he pointed to where the creek mingled with
the waters of the bay and where there was a patch
of yellow, "and you'll begin to go down and down.
First, you think it'll be easy to pull your feet out
but it ain't. You sink deeper and deeper and if
they's nobody around to throw you a rope you may
sink out of sight." He paused to give them time
to realize that danger. "Or if you don't you get
so all-fired tired with trying to pull yourself loose
that you fall over and then the tide comes in and
covers you up. So if the quicksands don't get you
the tide does and it's about the same—it's death!"

"Oh, how horrible!" murmured Thally.

"But it didn't happen," said Carol, more
brightly.

"Thanks to your warning," added Cecy, with
real appreciation.

"Yes. I seen you in time as I was coming down
to bait and load up my lobster pots. I'm going to
set 'em first thing in the morning. But it's a wonder to me Jensen didn't say something about these
sands. I take it you've seen and talked to him if
you're staying at Moaning Cliff?" he questioned.

"Yes, we talked to him," said Carol. "But he
said nothing about these sands. If we had known
they were so dangerous——"

"Well, they be—take my word for it. I guess

Jensen must have forgot. He knows about the land. He was 'most caught once—soon after he and his wife first come here. Well, be careful, that's all I got to say. Though it's queer about Jensen and his wife."

The lobsterman with a shake of his head started back to his pots. Carol, looking up toward the top of the cliff, saw two figures silhouetted there against the light. They were the figures of Emil Jensen and his wife looking curiously down at the girls.

The lobsterman also looked up, saw Jensen and his wife and, pointing what seemed an accusing finger at them, remarked:

"They had a right to tell you about this quicksand—they sure had!"

"I agree with you," called Carol. "And I shall speak to him about it. Very careless of him!"

She glanced again at the two on the high cliff. Jensen suddenly caught his wife by the arm, pulled her back and in a moment they were gone.

CHAPTER VI

THREATS AND SUSPICIONS

THE lobsterman with a final warning about the dangerous sands turned to go back to his pots and his boat.

"I don't like it here—let's go up," suggested Thally.

"Yes," agreed Cecy. "If there's dangerous sand beneath our feet there may be bats or something else deadly around our heads."

"I am anxious to have a talk with Jensen," declared Carol seriously. She picked up a large stone and tossed it to the middle of the shimmering, yellow stretch of sands. The rock remained for a moment on the top and then slowly began to sink out of sight. It seemed to struggle against being thus engulfed but in less than half a minute it was out of sight—the water and sand had closed over it with a murmuring gurgle.

"Horrible!" breathed Thally as they had watched it. "Think of being sucked down like that. Oh, I don't like it here at all!"

"Don't get cold feet and desert!" begged Cecy, half joking.

"Oh, I won't do that. I'll stick with Carol to the last ghost, but I won't come near those sands."

"None of us intend to test out the fisherman's story, I guess," Carol remarked. "It looks too true to be interesting in that way."

They made their way back to the top of the cliff. It was not an easy climb and took some time. There was no sight of Jensen or his wife when they reached the summit. They rested a few minutes, and then went on to the house where they found Rachel busy about getting lunch. More time had elapsed than they had realized. A boy called to sell a "mess of soft clams for chowder," and was hard to get rid of, and that took more time.

At lunch Carol told the housekeeper about their experience on the beach and warned her against the sands.

"Don't worry, Carol-love, I won't go near them," Rachel promised. "I expect to be pretty busy around this house. I never saw such an old, rambling place and it has——"

She suddenly looked at Carol, remembered their experience of the night and went out of the room with an exclamation about looking at something she had cooking on the stove. So neither Cecy nor Thally noticed her little distraction.

Suddenly there was heard the sound of voices at the back door. Rachel was evidently answering questions. She hurried into the dining room, through the big old-fashioned butler's pantry, a flushed look on her face, to say:

"It's that caretaker. I told him you were at lunch, but he——"

"Look here!" suddenly called out Emil Jensen who had rudely followed Rachel. His voice was blustering—threatening. "Look here! We're going to leave—my wife and I!"

"Leave!" Carol faltered.

"Yes. We don't want to be talked about and accused. We're through. Nobody is going to throw suspicions on us. We're leaving as soon as we can pack—today!"

"Oh, not today!" put in Mrs. Jensen who had followed her husband. "Not today, Emil!"

"Yes! Today! Nobody is going to suspect us! We're through!"

Carol, Cecy and Thally exchanged glances. They were glances of surprise not unmixed with consternation. There was no denying that the half-told stories about Moaning Cliff had gotten on their nerves in spite of the fact that absolutely nothing had happened during the first night of their stay. Carol and Rachel had their own little experience still secret. There had been a sense of security against harm and danger in the fact that almost within call was a sturdy man and his little less sturdy wife. For the caretakers were of a hardy race, a race not afraid of physical danger.

Now, almost at the very outset of the girls' stay in the mansion that had such a sinister reputation, this man and his wife were threatening to go away. What would the girls do?

Carol was the first to speak following the ultimatum of Emil Jensen.

"You surely can't mean this," she said.

"Yes, I do, Miss Duncan," he answered, and there was less of respect than of determination in his voice.

"But why?" asked Cecy, deciding it was time she gave Carol some backing.

"I told you!" Jensen almost snarled. "We're not going to be talked about and have suspicious fingers pointed at us. No! We're going." He turned abruptly and all but stamped his foot.

"But *we* haven't talked about you!" declared Thally, in a panic.

"Certainly not!" added Carol. "Anyhow, what would we talk about you for? What are *you* supposed to have done?"

"Well, maybe you haven't talked about us yet," said Mrs. Jensen, "but others have—not out in the open but behind our backs—in the village." She was deeply offended.

"That's it!" snapped her husband. "It's been done before and it's being done now. I told my wife the last time we heard these rumors that the *next* time would be the last and we'd quit. We're going. You can tell your aunt so. She don't owe us nothin' and we don't owe her nothin'. We're all squared up so we'll get out as fast as we can—today!"

"Not today, Emil," said Mrs. Jensen again.

"Yes. You said you was afraid to stay here much longer."

"Well, I am, in a way. But one more day won't hurt, I guess. And I got to pack my things. Besides—" she paused and looked significantly at the girls. Then she asked in a low voice:

"Did anything happen last night—I mean here, in the house?"

"No, not a thing," said Carol. She and Rachel exchanged quick, secret glances.

"Do you mean the moans—strange noises?" asked Cecy.

"Yes, that's it." Mrs. Jensen looked sharply at her husband but he did not glance at her.

"Certainly nothing happened," said Carol truthfully enough. "But is that what you mean—people have been saying you had something to do with the troubles here?"

"Not *exactly* saying it—just *suspicioning* it," particularized Jensen. "We hear the rumors and we see fingers being pointed at us like this morning. Why, you girls pointed at us yourselves but we couldn't hear what you said."

"Pointed at you?" Carol questioned in surprise. "Why——"

"When you was talking to Jed Bailey down on

the beach," interrupted Jensen. "I saw you———"

An understanding came to Carol. "Oh!" she exclaimed. "You mean when you were up here on the cliff. Yes, we saw you and we were talking about you, but it had nothing to do with the disturbances that are said to be around here. But we did talk about you to the lobsterman," she finished, hoping to make the man understand.

"I thought so!" sniffed Mrs. Jensen.

"But it was about quite another subject," Carol proceeded. "Jed Bailey was saying it was strange you did not warn us about the quicksands. We might have been caught there. We were going to walk across them when he warned us. It did seem that you might have done so for surely you know. Bailey said we could have been swallowed up there."

Quick looks were exchanged between husband and wife. Then the countenance of Emil Jensen underwent a change for the better.

"Was that why you pointed at us?" he asked.

"Of course!" declared Cecy. "It seems careless of you and your wife not to have warned us," she kept insisting.

"It was!" frankly admitted the caretaker. "I told my wife to mention it to you, but I guess you didn't, Mona," he said, and his air of resentment melted like snow in the sun.

"No, I forgot it," admitted Mrs. Jensen. "But I thought you would remember and do it. I never gave it another thought, what with wondering if everything else was all right up here. It was careless of us and we're sorry. I guess we won't go away now, Emil," she changed her mind suddenly. She showed she meant what she was saying this time.

"No, I guess we won't. I beg your pardons," he went on. "It was all a mistake." He clasped and unclasped his hands as if nervously glad to be able to stay. The indignation seemed to have grown out of the imagined insult of old Jed Bailey.

"All right," assented Carol, much relieved herself. "But while we are on the subject, let me ask —have the village people been casting suspicions on you about the weird happenings here?"

"Yes, they have!" snapped Mrs. Jensen. "Nasty, gossiping folk they are. Why, we haven't any more to do with the noises than you have."

"There haven't been any noises yet," laughed Cecy. "And when we hear any we're going to find out what makes them. You see if we don't."

"Others have tried that but didn't get very far," said the caretaker with a gloomy air. "But if you care to stay we'll keep on as we were and look after the place for your aunt, and do all we can for you."

"That will be fine!" Carol answered. "Then those sands are really dangerous?" she asked.

"At times, yes, at times," Jensen admitted. "When the tide's just right they are. Best keep off 'em at all times. You got to know the state of the water to cross 'em in safety. Keep away, that's best."

"We shall," promised Cecy.

Jensen and his wife departed in a more lively mood than they had come in with, but they left the girls wondering just the same.

"What do you think that all meant?" Thally asked when they had a chance to talk after lunch.

"You mean Jensen?" inquired Carol.

"Yes. Do you think he and his wife are playing a game—a trick—or what is it?"

"If they were up to tricks," was Cecy's opinion, "I don't believe they would be as open about threatening to leave as they were."

"Probably not," Carol agreed. "But yet, there is something about this I don't quite see, and I don't like it. But we came here to solve this mystery for Aunt Isabel and we're going to do it. For the time matters are smoothed over. Nothing has happened; nothing may happen. So let's try to forget about it and enjoy our vacation here."

"That's the spirit!" exclaimed Thally with her usual mockery. "And when Glenn and Ted come over—if they ever do—and when Rosie gets here —by the way when is she coming, Carol?" she asked suddenly.

"She may descend upon us any time. You know what Rosie is for sudden appearances."

"Yes. Well, when she comes we'll surely have some jolly times."

"You haven't been your usual jolly self, Thally, since we got here," chided Cecy. "Why wait for Rosie?"

"Oh, well, Rosie is young. And now what shall we do?" She looked at Carol. "These moments are growing longer and longer," she pointed out.

"I think we should explore this house," came Carol's decisive answer. "It's only logical to do so now. We have come to the old mansion which has an evil reputation, whether deserved or not. If there are unearthly noises they must come either from within or without the house. Am I right so far?" she paused to ask.

"As rain, or whatever is rightest!" admitted Cecy.

"Now, if we look this place over thoroughly we may find out some simple explanation for the sudden leaving of the various tenants and all this sensitiveness of our Jensens. How about it, girls?"

"Right again!" said Thally. "Lead, Carol, me lad!" and they jumped up to follow the leader.

"Begin at the top!" suggested Cecy, which they had already started out to do.

Heading for the attic with their flashlights they laughed and joked, inviting all hidden ghosts to come forth and get acquainted. Cecy tried to stop Thally from "tempting fate," but she did a little tempting herself. They found the attic was a most picturesque place. Tucked away in dim and cobwebbed corners were fascinating relics of a bygone day, which, breathlessly, the girls poked about in.

There was a quaint spinning wheel, the kind with the large wheel that was to be turned by hand for the spinning of wool. There was also the more commonly seen small flax-wheel with the treadle for foot power. Here and there were old trunks, some open and spilling out their contents of old newspapers and magazines. In one corner, where Thally poked herself without a light, she was suddenly startled by a musical jingling of bells. She exclaimed in fright but Carol and Cecy laughed.

"I didn't think these existed any more outside of a theatre playing The Old Homestead," said Carol, shaking the string of bells that were worn by horses pulling a sleigh over the silent snow.

"And look here!" exclaimed Cecy, bringing forward from another corner, where the spiders had abandoned their webs, a strange object in the shape of many tin tubes fastened in a frame. "What in the world is this?"

"Candle-mould," declared Thally. "I've seen one like it in my grandmother's house. This place must be as old as hers was. What relics for a collector!" she exclaimed in admiration as she looked about the attic and saw some real antique furniture although most of it in sad state of decay.

"There is a lot of junk here!" agreed Cecy, as they saw old brass warming pans, and ancient kerosene lamps, some used before the advent of glass chimneys when two wicks drawn up through two metal tubes gave a smoky light. Also there were some flint-lock muskets and rifles as well as more modern, but still old weapons and some swords, hanging high on strong wooden pegs.

"If we can drive the haunt away from Moaning Cliff, girls," Cecy went on, "maybe Aunt Isabel will let us open an antique shop here for her. Wouldn't that be great?"

"That's one thing I've always wanted to operate," said Carol. "This attic is a dear place," she murmured. "So quaint—such lovely old things."

The attic certainly was all of that and contained much that might have been valued by a collector. But as for containing anything that could be associated with ghosts, haunts or the making of weird noises—nothing was turned up that could possibly be connected with the mystery.

"We drew a blank here," admitted Carol as they descended. "Now for the next floor."

"And I'm hoping we'll find nothing down where we sleep!" murmured Cecy.

They found nothing there, nor anything in the tower room, either, for the ancient house had the style of architecture that included a tower, though the rooms in the half circle were dim, dusty and unused. In one was a great chest closed and fastened with massive padlocks.

"We must open that some day," Carol decided, "if we have to get Jensen to pry it open. And now we'll try the first floor. That ought to be easy."

They went from room to room, starting with the closed "parlor," with its horsehair furniture and a "whatnot" in a corner, filled with various objects from a little lead coffin with a miniature grinning ivory skull in it, to a bottle containing strata of various colored sands that had been picked up as a souvenir from the Grand Canyon, as a written label stated.

But they saw nothing suspicious and heard not an unusual sound.

"There's only the cellar left," said Cecy. "Do we have to go down there?"

"Of course!" declared Carol. "That's the most likely place for ghosts."

"Oh, stop it!" demanded Thally. "I'm not going down!"

"Why, Thal! The old brave! What's happened to your nerve? You can't back out now!" laughed Cecy. "Besides, it's broad daylight and we have our torches. Come on!" shouted the one usually most timid.

"Be a sport!" urged Carol, for Thally was hesitating.

"All right," conceded Thally with a sigh of resignation. "But we ought to take Rachel with us. She has no nerves she boasts."

The housekeeper assented with a laugh and all four of them descended to the cellar.

Just as they started for the cellar, Carol and Rachel exchanged quick glances. Not a word was said but each one understood. It was a renewal of the pledge they had taken that first night to say nothing about what they had heard.

But after all, the housekeeper might have had the nightmare.

It was large, damp, cool and dark and was divided by partitions of brick and wood, into several sections. There was a laundry beneath the kitchen and near it what seemed to be a little room set apart.

"Wine bin," said Carol as she opened the door and saw the racks for bottles, all empty now. "I have heard Aunt Isabel say her grandfather was very fond of his bottles."

"Or what came out of them!" laughed Cecy. "Ugh! But this is a queer, rambling old place," she said in a low voice as she flashed her light about cautiously.

"Come on, we must finish the job," Carol hurried them.

They walked toward the front of the cellar, Carol and Cecy in the lead. Suddenly Cecy caught her sister's arm and whispered:

"What's that?"

"Where?" Carol's voice was also a whisper.

"Over in that corner." She pointed to one in the extreme dim and shadowy confines of the place. Then she focused her light there. There was no doubt of it.

Something was moving in the corner!

CHAPTER VII

MOANS IN THE NIGHT

"WHAT is it?" whispered Thally as, walking beside Rachel, she came close up behind Carol.

"I don't know," Carol answered cautiously.

"Something in the corner—an animal, maybe," supplied Cecy. "Oh, it must be a big animal," she gasped. "Maybe a bear——"

"Oh!" half screamed Thally, grabbing Carol impulsively.

"Easy, easy," cautioned Rachel who was making her way toward the corner.

But a moment later the fear and suspense ended simultaneously. For the dim, shadowy and bulky figure that Cecy's electric torch had half disclosed in the dark corner came forward into the full glare of three flashlights now turned upon it and was revealed as Emil Jensen!

"Oh!" gasped Carol and her exclamation of surprise and relief mingled was echoed by the others. "Oh—what—what are you doing down here?" She strove to make her voice accusing and sternly interrogatory. "Why are you here?" Rachel was trying to quiet her.

"I'm looking for rat holes!" announced the care-taker sharply.

"Rat holes!" It was said at once, by all four, both an exclamation of surprise as well as question.

"Rat holes," repeated Jensen with a chuckle. He had a flashlight in his hand but it was not show-ing its light. Rats are known to be very wary of danger signals.

"I shut my light off soon as I heard you coming and saw the reflections of yours," he stated as he glanced down at his torch. "I didn't want to miss rats or waste my batteries."

"Then you knew we were coming?" asked Cecy suspiciously.

"I knew it was you soon as I heard feet," said the man. "I didn't figure it could be anybody else down here this time of day."

"Might there be somebody down here at night?" asked Carol quickly.

"At night?" His surprise was evident.

"Yes."

"No. Not as I knows of—only rats. I'm look-ing for their holes to stop 'em up with broken glass." He held up a bottle. "Got it from the old wine cellar," he said. "I was going to bust it if I found a hole and stuff the glass in. Rats don't like broken glass."

"Did you find any?" asked Thally, keeping close to Carol.

"Can't say I did. Not even a hole, so I'll save

this bottle," and he laughed a little rather foolishly.

"But how did you get down here without any of us seeing you?" asked Carol. "And why did you pick this time to hunt for rat holes? Is there a time——"

"I came down through the outside cellar door, as I often do," he interrupted. "Oh, it's kept locked," he quickly added. "Don't worry about that. I have another key. The other hangs up above the kitchen sink," he told Rachel. "I didn't bother to tell you I was coming here to look for rats' nests," he proceeded. "Thought it might bother you. So I just slipped in and I'd have slipped out again if you hadn't caught me," he chuckled. "How'd you know I was here? I didn't make any noise to speak of." Again he chuckled.

"We didn't hear you," Cecy said. "We were going over the whole house, looking for some explanation of the strange noises——"

"Which we are merely wondering about," broke in Carol.

"Well, maybe you won't hear any," said the caretaker. "'Tisn't everybody that does. Your aunt did, though," he said with a shake of his head.

"So we understand," said Carol, rather coldly. "But we were investigating the whole place from attic to cellar, and so came down here to finish up."

"And you didn't find anything?" he asked.

"Only you!" said Cecy, sharply.

"Oh, well, I don't count, miss. And I didn't find any rat holes either."

"You were looking for them, specially?" asked Thally.

"Yes, miss. To tell you the truth, after I got thinking about it and talking it over with my wife, I had a notion that maybe it was rats that had been making the noises. I told my wife so and she said I should come here and look for holes. But there aren't any. Not one, so you needn't worry. I guess girls don't like rats," he finished.

"Nor mice, either!" said Thally decidedly. "I'm glad we haven't any."

"Oh, I wouldn't guarantee there aren't any *mice!*" Again the caretaker chuckled. "But I'll stake my reputation on there being no rats. So you can sleep in peace. Now I'll be going."

"Well—thanks for coming over," Carol managed to say. But something else was on her mind. So she asked: "As far as you know who was the first one in this place to hear the strange noises; my aunt?"

"No, it was before her time," the man replied. "Soon after she came in charge of the place, all furnished as you see it now, she decided to rent it, as it was ordered in the will that she must make a moneyed use of it in order to keep it. So she lent it to Dr. Mandell. He come here with some of his patients, making it a sort of rest cure and like-a-that. But something went wrong. Whether it was the noises or not I can't say. Anyhow, one of his patients died and then another was killed."

"Killed here?" exclaimed the three girls as one.

"Well, he killed himself—with a rope—down in this cellar—from that beam over there. I helped cut him down," said Mr. Jensen with obvious pride. "Things like that don't bother me. Yes, the poor man killed himself."

They all involuntarily moved toward the stairs.

"Ugh!" groaned Cecy, "worse and worse!"

"A man hanged himself in *this* cellar!" Rachel repeated. "Girls, we must go up——"

"Was it because he was scared or something?" breathed Thally.

"Oh, no. He was out of his head. He'd probably done the same thing wherever he was. You can't blame this place for that. But I'm just telling you what happened. After that word got around and of course the other patients heard of it, and what with the queer noises and all Dr. Mandell gave it up. 'Twas after that Miss Duncan come here but she couldn't stand it either."

"My dears, we must go upstairs," insisted Rachel quietly. The memory of a hanged man in the old cellar was surely not wholesome to dwell upon.

They paused in the back hall, having made Jensen lock his door and come upstairs as they had gone down.

Then Carol again took up her line of questioning.

"And no one else has since been able to live in the place?" she asked the man.

"Well, miss, you've about got the right of it," the caretaker admitted. "Nobody has. But no amount of noises would bother me. Besides, I'd figure they were worth putting up with in order to keep this place. For you know—I guess your aunt told you—if she don't soon put it to profitable use she's likely to lose it. I don't know all the ins and outs of the law, but that's about it."

"So we understand," said Cecy. "That's why we're here."

"And we're going to find out what the real trouble is," declared Carol.

"Well, I hope you do. Sort of mysterious, if you ask me. I've heard 'em off and on, when the tenants would call me to come in at the middle of the night to listen to 'em. But I never could figure out what made 'em. I don't believe it could be the man who hanged himself. Because he was a mild, nice sort of little gentleman and——"

"Oh, will you stop talking about it!" nervously gasped Thally.

"Yes, of course, miss. But I thought you wanted to know and——"

"I think we have heard enough," Carol said. "Thank you."

"And you can depend there ain't no rats!" finished the caretaker as he started for the door.

The girls and Rachel waited until he had closed

the door. "Well!" exclaimed Thally as she put away her flashlight, "all I can say is worse and more of it."

"What is worse?" asked Cecy.

"Finding that man down cellar."

"Oh, I think that was all right," reasoned Carol. "After all there might have been rats. I'm glad there aren't!"

"So am I," said Thally, "and I'm glad *we* didn't find the hanged man," she attempted to joke. "But I don't like Emil Jensen."

"Nor I," agreed Cecy.

"I'm not going to form an opinion yet," declared Carol. "I want to wait and see what happens."

"When?" asked the others. Rachel had left them. As usual her protective presence had given them all courage in the cellar trip.

"Tonight might be the night," said Carol as she started toward her room. "And now enough of haunts. I'm going for a swim!"

"It will do us all good!" agreed Cecy. "And I have the niftiest bathing suit, with the open back and bridle effect. It's fetching."

"I suppose you think it will fetch Glenn or some of the boys," mocked Thally.

"Well, frankly, yes. I'm said to be easy to look at!"

"Cecy!" chided Carol.

"Oh, well, so are you both, so don't get jealous!" Cecy laughed.

It was delightful in the calm waters of the bay where real swimming was easier than in the more turbulent ocean. The girls dipped in, came out to dry on the beach, walked as close as was safe to the sinister quicksands, and then repeated the dip. So passed most of the day and they were much refreshed and in better spirits when they had supper on the cool, screened-in porch.

"Well, here's to a good night!" gaily chanted Cecy as, some time later, they went to bed. First, however, they had made a survey of the old house with their lights trained on dark corners. All was quiet and in order.

"And so to bed! as Mr. Pepys would say," drawled Thally as she switched on the light in her room.

It was Carol who awakened later and found the time to be soon after midnight. The day's swimming, the long hours in the ozoned air and the general peace of the place had sent them all soundly to sleep soon after they went to bed. But Carol had awakened; she was wide awake now.

At first she could not understand what had roused her. She had been dreaming, rather pleasantly, so it was no alarm from that source. But as she opened her eyes, and saw, dimly, the objects in her room (for there was a low light glowing in the hall) she suddenly realized what had aroused her.

Throughout the whole ancient house was echoing the most strange and weird sound! It was low and deep. It seemed to come from the very depths of the foundations. It was unmistakably a moan, and no nightmare cry. A moan that began with a high, piercing note as: "Ohohohooooo!" and deepened into a half sob of terrible despair.

"Ohohohoooooo! Ugh-ugh-ugh! Ahahahaaaa-aah! Oh-mmmmmmmm!"

With trembling fingers Carol reached for the flashlight beneath her pillow.

CHAPTER VIII

DEEPER MYSTERY

WHETHER it was the noise of the moans which now seemed to fill the whole house, or the crash, as Carol's trembling fingers dropped her flashlight on the floor beside her bed, that awakened Cecy and Thally, was not clear. At any rate both girls sat up suddenly in the darkness and called:

"What is it?"

"I don't know," was Carol's reply as she leaned over the side of her bed and groped for the fallen light. "But didn't you hear it?"

"I heard a thump," said Cecy, unwilling to admit anything else.

"That was my light—I dropped it," Carol called again, wondering how far beneath her bed the perverse little electric torch had rolled. "But the other noises—don't you hear them even now? There!"

Cecy and Thally would have been deaf, indeed, if they did not hear the groans that now seemed louder than ever. Carol in her nervousness, unable to reach her torch, called:

"Can one of you make a light? I can't reach mine."

"Here I come!" announced Cecy, and a moment later a wavering beam of illumination along the hall showed that she was approaching Carol's door. A second later another dancing point of light indicated that Thally was also on her way up the line.

The two girls flashed their torches on pretty, disheveled Carol sitting up in bed, her eyes wide with wonder and not with terror, and her hair fluffed about her face.

The three girls waited, listened in tense silence. Then the silence was broken by another series of echoing groans and weird, uncanny moans, louder than before.

"Oh, what is it?" cried Thally instinctively crouching down beside Carol.

"It's worse than Aunt Isabel ever told us to expect!" wailed Cecy. "I think she was terrible to get us into a place like this!" Her voice shook with sheer terror.

"So far it isn't anything but noises," said Carol, made braver by the presence of the others. "Noises never hurt anyone."

"Don't they? Well, the noise-makers might. And nerves!" exclaimed Cecy. "Mine are all shot already."

"I don't see how we can stand it," said Thally, usually so bold. "I think we ought to get out of here." Her face was white enough to show off those freckles now.

"And not solve the mystery?" demanded Carol.

"But it's somehow so sort of substantial," declared Thally.

"No wind nor other little thing could ever make that noise," added Cecy.

A soft patting step brought Rachel to join them. She was flaunting her own particular flashlight and wearing a pretty lavender kimono.

"Wide awake, girls!" she said. "Did you hear anything—a noise I mean?"

"Did we?" cried Cecy, springing up like a jack-knife.

"As if we could miss it," echoed Thally. "Rachel, I'm going to sleep in that other bed in your room the rest of the night. I'm cold scared."

"Nonsense!" broke in Carol. "It isn't really anything dangerous. Wait! Listen! The noises have stopped! It's gone!"

It was true. The groans, the wails and the moaning sounds had all ceased. The girls looked wonderingly at one another.

"I heard a kind of thump," said Rachel, vaguely. She didn't want to add to their alarm.

"That was me. I dropped my flashlight," Carol explained. She was out of bed now and getting down deliberately on the floor she poked her head under the bed and came out with the flashlight.

"But there were other, awful noises," said

Thally. "Didn't you hear them, Rachel?"

"The most weird sounds," added Cecy, almost hissing the words.

"I heard dogs howling," insisted the housekeeper.

"Dogs!" cried Thally.

"If those were dogs they must be the ghosts of the legendary ones that Charon, or somebody, threw a sop to, whatever a sop is," remarked Cecy, jumbling her mythology.

"It *was* dogs," declared Rachel with finality. "I know a dog howl when I hear it. Some dogs have got in the cellar and they can't get out. I'm going down and let them out or they'll be howling all night."

"Oh, no Rachel——"

"You mustn't go down there alone."

"It's simply suicidal," each of the three had protestingly exclaimed.

"I tell you it's dogs," the housekeeper declared again. "And we'll have to let them out if we want any sleep tonight. Who's coming?"

They could not hold back after this. There were four of them, Carol was saying, and with their lights and Rachel's courage perhaps it was better to go right down now. Rachel led the way downstairs and toward the inside cellar-way. The old, big house was now quiet, save for the padding footsteps of bedroom slippers of the investigators. The moans had not sounded again although the girls kept listening for them.

It was not until they reached the inside cellar door that Carol remembered something. She said:

"How could any dogs get in the cellar? It's locked inside and out. Jensen saw to that."

"I don't care about that," protested Rachel. "There are dogs in this cellar. They howled. They are quiet now because they heard us coming —or scent us. Likely they got in a window that was overlooked. I'll soon scat them." She was now armed with a clothes stick she had snatched from the stairway shelf, and she gave it a resounding tap.

"Do you scat a dog?" asked Cecy in a low voice of Thally. "I thought scats were the exclusive properties of cats."

"Oh, I don't know. This is so awful," murmured Thally, for indeed a mid-night descent into that dark cavernous cellar was all of *"awful."*

"I know," admitted Cecy, grasping Thally by the arm.

"It's sic!" half exploded the ebullient Cecy. "I mean, you sic a dog and you scat a cat. It's good to know." As if it mattered.

"Please don't talk so much," warned Carol as they neared the inner cellar door. "If there is something or someone down there making noises, we want to catch them in the act and not have them——"

"Oh, I don't want to *catch* anyone!" protested Thally. "All I want is peace and quiet and to be allowed to sleep without groans." She was standing still now. Thally Bond did not like this adventure.

"But they've stopped!" said Carol, as if in triumphant vindication of some theory she had been holding to.

Then, as if to mock her, while the four were grouped around the door, the groans came again, loud, vibrating and haunting:

"Ohhhhh! OO-oooooo! Ahhhhh! Ugggg!"

Thally was so startled, she jumped back and almost knocked Cecy over. But the ever faithful and dependable Rachel caught her and held her upright. Carol, who had been about to open the door, drew back quickly.

"I'm not going down in that cellar, four of us or not four of us, lights or no lights—without a man!" declared Thally as the moans ceased.

"A man!" faltered Carol.

"Yes. Let's go get that caretaker, Hansen, Ransen or whatever his name is. He said he'd help us. Let's go get him."

"Well—" faltered Carol. She, herself, seemed glad enough to agree.

"I really think it would be best," panted Cecy as if every one didn't know she thought so.

"All right," agreed her sister. "Rachel——"

"We don't need a man!" objected the sturdy Scotch housekeeper. "But if it makes you all feel any better——"

"I won't stir another step without a man!" was Thally's ultimatum.

"All right," Carol assented. They turned away from the still locked door, paused to listen, but heard nothing alarming and, a few moments later, were out in the night's darkness, illuminated by the stars, a quarter moon and their own flashlights. It was very still and quiet. Only the distant booming of the surf and the softer lapping of the waves of the bay on the sand broke the stillness. Glad to be safely out of doors they started down the lane that led from Rocky Cliff to the gate-house.

Emil Jensen proved that he spoke the truth when he said he was a light sleeper. The girls had no need of throwing pebbles at his bedroom window, nor did they need to pound on his door. As they walked up the gravel path leading to the little cottage a voice called from a window:

"Who is it?"

"Oh, Jensen!" exclaimed Carol. "We have heard the moans!"

"Rats!" exclaimed the caretaker.

"What!" demanded Carol, indignantly. "I told you——"

"I know you did, miss. And I mean it was probably rats you heard. There must be some holes of 'em in the cellar after all."

"All the rats in the world couldn't make the noises we heard," called out Cecy and her voice was tense and solemn. "It was awful!"

"Like some moaning in death," intoned Thally.

"You said you'd come if we needed you," Carol reminded him.

"And so I will—glad to do it. But you'll find nothing. No one ever has. Just a moment. That's the way it goes. We've tried it time and time again. But wait; I'll get ready."

A light gleamed now in the upper window. It flickered about and presently Mr. Jensen came down; plainly he had dressed in a great hurry, and as he mumbled answers he seemed but half awake.

"I thought it was about time you heard something," he then said pointedly, swinging his kerosene lantern as they started back to the house.

"Why, do those noises come at certain times?" asked Carol.

"No, there's no certainty about 'em, except you hear 'em at night. I don't know why. Of course I'll go down cellar with you but you find nothing. I know; I've looked before."

"How do you know about this time?" asked Carol.

"I've been down before and this time ain't no different," he chuckled. "You'll see."

They were soon within the house again. They entered the rear door, passed through the kitchen and were soon in the back hall out of which opened the inner cellar door. Even as they entered, the moans sounded again, but not so loud, rather faintly.

"Yes, that's the moans all right," said Jensen, more cheerfully than the girls thought necessary. "Now we'll see."

"See what?" demanded Cecy sharply.

"See nothing if it turns out as it always has," he grumbled.

They opened the cellar door, flashed their lights down the stairs and soon the girls and Rachel were following Jensen into the black and damp depths. There was light enough now—no one could complain of lack of illumination. But when they entered the cellar they found absolutely nothing. And the sounds did not echo again.

Jensen flashed his lantern and the girls focused their electric torches into every nook and corner, but there was not a sign to indicate how the sounds had been made.

"Well, I certainly thought there were dogs," declared Rachel in surprise.

"We didn't look in the old wine cellar," said Cecy suddenly.

But that, too, was a void. And the outer door was securely locked and every window was nailed shut. There was not a sign of any break in the impregnable cellar.

"I told you; didn't I?" sneered Jensen.

What could it have been? No suspicions now, no longer any doubt about those groans and yet— they found nothing!

CHAPTER IX

ROSIE TAKES A BOW

HAVING completed the survey and found nothing to indicate what had caused the weird and ghostly noises, the girls, the housekeeper and Jensen came up stairs and stood for a few minutes in the back hall-way.

Jensen was the first to speak following a rather long silence.

"Well?" he asked.

"I suppose there is nothing more to do," Carol admitted. "We haven't found out anything."

"But we did hear moans," said Thally with a little shiver.

"Didn't you hear them, Jensen?" asked Cecy defiantly.

"Who, me, miss? And me away off in the cottage? No, I didn't hear a thing until you come and got me out of bed."

"Are you a sound sleeper?" asked the housekeeper.

"No, I'm not!" he almost snapped. "Why?"

"I should think almost anybody within a quarter of a mile, on a still night like this, could have heard those dogs howling," she went on.

"What dogs?" asked Jensen.

"The ones that were howling in the cellar."

"Hum!" he mumbled. "Dogs, eh? Well, I might say rats but I don't even say that. Didn't see any rats scurry away when we came down. As for dogs, how'd they get in and out?" He seemed to think he had asked the housekeeper an unanswerable question. But Rachel had her own ideas.

"I don't know how they got in or out," she announced, "but dogs were in this cellar and I know it. I know a dog's howls, though they don't mean anything to me as they do to some folks—a message of death," she finished. It was a long speech for Rachel.

"Oh, stop it! Stop it!" begged Thally, her hands going to her ears in an effort to shut out unpleasant news. But she was able to cover only one ear for she still held her flashlight and she made such a funny appearance trying to hold the torch in a few fingers, and get at least one other into the least protected ear, that the others laughed, even Jensen condescending to smile though rather sourly.

"I don't care how I look!" announced Thally. "I don't like this ghost business and if it's going to keep up——"

"Don't say you'll go home," begged Cecy, catching a hint of such a threat in Thally's voice.

"Well, I'll feel inclined that way if we have to get up every night to investigate moans and then not find any."

"You can't find a moan," Cecy reminded them foolishly.

"Well, you know what I mean." Thally was tired and showed it.

"It is too bad," declared Carol. "I know just how you feel, Thally. I'm sorry. Of course, Cecy and I must keep faith with Aunt Isabel. We said we'd do our best to get at the bottom of this mystery and we shall. But it wouldn't be right to inflict on you——"

"Who's inflicting anything on me?" snapped Thally, becoming more like her normal self now. "And if you think I'm going to desert you, why, guess again. I'll stick it out," she ended defiantly.

"Well, if that's all for tonight I'll be getting back to bed. Unless you're afraid and want me to stay the rest of the night," Jensen added with a chuckle. "I can get my wife over——"

"It won't be necessary, thank you," said Carol a bit coldly. "We'll be all right, now, I'm sure."

And they were. For the remainder of the night passed peacefully and quietly with not so much as an uncanny whisper to disturb the silence of the old mansion. All the sounds heard, before the girls fell into rather uneasy slumbers, were the usual noises of the night, made by crickets, tree-toads or other nocturnal creatures. But tired girls are sound sleepers.

Next morning Cecy burst into Carol's room soon after Rachel had gone down stairs to start breakfast, as evidenced by the aroma of coffee and bacon, floating upward.

"Carol, I know just what it is!" Cecy gasped, shaking her pretty, fluffy hair out of her blue eyes.

"What—what is?" asked Carol, rather vaguely.

"What made those groaning noises. It came to me all at once just as I awoke. It's all so simple."

"Well, what is it?" asked her sister. "Tell me and then relate it to Thally. She needs to be re-assured."

"It's wireless!" announced Cecy triumphantly as she perched on the foot of Carol's bed, her hands clasped about her knees for all the world like a most artistic separated book-end.

"Wireless!" repeated Carol, indifferently.

"Yes. You know, radio. Some distant station, where the difference in time makes it daylight there or early evening when it's midnight here, has been broadcasting a series of radio thrillers, detective stories, drama or what have you. At certain times the villain or the victim or somebody groans and moans and indicates anguish. The sounds are picked up here and we hear them. That's all. Isn't it simple?"

"It would be if that were the explanation," Carol agreed. "But though there are many things in this old house, a wireless receiving set isn't among them. In lots of ways I'm glad of it, for though the machines are a blessing at times, too much wire-less is worse than not enough. I don't see how you

could figure out, Cecy, that we could get wireless
sounds without a radio in the house."

"Pooh! Simple, my child. I've often read that
under certain circumstances water pipes, a mesh bed
spring, or even the steel ribs of umbrellas will act
as— Oh, I don't know the real word—but aerial
is what it amounts to. I read that once a man lying
in bed heard beautiful music. He didn't have a
radio but his bed spring picked up distant sounds
and he got them."

"I don't believe such a thing could happen," declared Carol.

"Wait until Glenn gets here and I'll prove it.
You'll see." Cecy was simply crowing over her
scientific solution of the mystery.

"Oh, Cecy! That would be impossible. Those
groans were so deep and vibrant that no radio I
ever heard could reproduce them. They were right
here—in the house, down cellar. All our ears
couldn't fooled. No, your explanation is interesting, darling, but I'm afraid we can't prove that our
ghostie is a crooner," Carol argued.

"Crooner or groaner, I'll bet it will turn out to
be. Glenn will know. Can't we go over and ask
him to help us? Camp Tagawah isn't so far away.
Besides maybe he doesn't know we are settled here
yet and he may be just dying to see *us*." She em-
phasized the *us,* because she should have said
"Carol."

"Well, we could ride over," Carol assented

slowly. "But it wouldn't be right to take him away from his camp duties. Remember he is being paid for staying there and besides he wants to make a good record."

"He will. Count on your Glenny for that." Cecy was feeling fine this morning. "But I guess he can get a little time off. Anyhow I'm anxious to have his opinion on this Dick-Dead-Eye stuff. And he can be free from camp at night, I imagine. He could come here then—that's when we need him; nights."

"We certainly did last night," Carol conceded. "But I hope the Terror has used up all its power for a while. But if going to see Glenn about it will make you feel easier— I mean, if he should support the radio theory———"

"Wouldn't that make *you* feel easier?" pursued Cecy.

"Well—perhaps, it would," Carol smilingly admitted.

Thally, hearing the talk, came sauntering in, wearing a beautiful pink robe; her face rosy from slumber. She seemed to have slept off her fright and nervousness of the night.

"What's going on?" she asked, with a half yawn.

"Oh, Cecy has a theory," began Carol, but she got no farther for her sister interrupted to tell it all over again. And it improved with repetition.

"I have read of such things," Thally admitted. "I only hope it's true. And it would be good to have Glenn's opinion anyhow. He's always so wise."

"The ayes have it!" laughed Carol. "We'll start for camp right after breakfast. And it's a good day for a drive."

Rachel said she was not in the least afraid to remain in the old, big house alone for a while, so, soon the girls were headed for Camp Tagawah, several miles away on the shores of Indian Lake.

On the way out they had passed the old mill on Rocky Cliff estate. The water in the pond was higher now, and quite a stream was running into and splashing from the half-ruined flume. At times the old wheel moved slightly.

And as the girls in the roadster swung past it, the wheel suddenly made a half turn, at the same time giving forth a doleful squeal which really came from the ungreased axle and bearings.

"Wait! Stop!" suddenly commanded Thally.

"What for?" asked Carol, putting on the brakes.

"Did you hear that noise?" went on Thally, her face flushing so that her freckles stood out bravely beneath her tan. "It was the mill wheel groaning! I'm sure that made the noises we heard in the night!"

"Oh, maybe it did—instead of radio?" Cecy was ever ready to adopt a new theory as long as it didn't seem dangerous.

"Nonsense!" asserted Carol. "I have heard the old wheel make a noise and I knew exactly what it was. But it was nothing like the noises of the night. And, besides, it is too far away from the house to have been heard there. But isn't it a picturesque old mill, though," Carol remarked as they paused to see if the wheel would groan or moan again. But it did not. "Soon we must take time out to explore this mill. If the ghosts don't hide here perhaps they—bathe in the pool!"

"Did you ever see a ghost in bathing?" chanted Thally. "Well, I'll never go in that musty old mill. It looks like a fine place for the miller's ghost, I'd say."

"Nothing more dangerous than moth-millers! I'll bet," laughed Carol as they drove along, the noise of their own car too much for any further echo of squeals from the mill.

They found Glenn and his chum Ted Morton taking a little rest on a home-made bench in front of a tent. After exclamations of joy and surprise, Glenn and Ted took their company to a more sheltered spot—the deserted camp kitchen.

"The youngsters all did pretty well today," Glenn said, "even Slim Brown had enough confidence to swim without his balloon tire. But I wouldn't want them to see three girls at one time. It might make trouble," he joked.

"They'd expect cake," drawled Ted. "Why do women always fetch cake? Don't they know anything about ants?"

"Why, Ted," lisped Cecy, "boys eat the cake

right up, don't they? Why leave crumbs for teeny-weeny ants?"

"Hey!" sang out Thally. "Let's talk sense. We came here, didn't we, to get the boys over to hunt ghosts?"

"Hunt ghosts!" cried Glenn gaily, when he heard what had happened. "We ask nothing better, do we, Pal?"

"Surest thing you know!" declared Ted. "We'll be over this very night!"

"And lay the ghost!" Glenn added, slapping his brown hands together in anticipation.

After further talk along that line, the girls were shown about the camp, meeting the matron and trained nurse who were stationed there.

"Stay to lunch?" Mrs. Brennen, the matron pressed cordially. "We are going to have creamed cod-fish, and *not* with sweetened condensed milk." It seemed the boys had made that sort of mistake when it had been their turn in the kitchen.

But the girls declined to stay and after renewed promises on the part of Glenn and Ted that they would arrive before dark and stay for the evening, and all night maybe, they started back.

"Now we'll find out something," enthused Cecy. "I don't trust that old Jensen. And I'll bet he knows more than he tells us."

"Well, if he does," declared Carol, "he has a fine way of keeping it to himself."

"I don't like him nor his wife, either," insisted Cecy.

"Well, I'm glad the boys are to be with us," said Thally, quietly.

Rachel, too, was glad to hear that the boys were coming, for she liked Glenn very much, and Carol insinuated she might even like Ted better. They were just settling down for a little rest after lunch when they heard a voice, a humming singing voice floating in the hall.

> "Oh, most jolly girls are we
> Sometimes four and sometimes three.
> From the dawn until the night——"

"It's Rosie!" cried Carol.

"Rosie's roundelay!" chirped Cecy, jumping up and rushing out to meet her friend.

"Oh, I'm so glad she's come!" breathed Thally as they all made for the big hall-way.

"Rosie, take a bow!" chanted Cecy, and then the fun was on.

CHAPTER X

THE BOYS STAY

AND that was Rosalind Wells—Rosie to her friends—who was thus singing her way into the old place and delighting every one there by her sudden appearance. But there was no question as to her welcome, and she was soon dancing merrily around with her chums, "as light as a soap bubble," to quote Cecy, amid a general exchange of hugs, kisses and such enthusiastic greetings.

"So you finally got here!" repeated Cecy. She and Rosie had been great friends as long as either knew what friendship meant.

"Yes, I got here," Rosie admitted, laughing again. In fact she was seldom without a smile or a laugh about her. The stock never seemed to run low. "And not so very late, either," she went on. "You haven't been here very long yourselves."

"No," said Thally in a low voice. "But long enough for things to have happened." Thally was plainly weakening on the adventure.

"Ahem!" quickly coughed Carol as she trod on Thally's foot and whispered: "Not yet, Thal."

"Oh!" exclaimed Thally. "I didn't——"

If Rosie gave any heed to this little byplay exchange she did not show it, for she was brimming over with life, gaiety and general happiness. Besides that, she seemed to have a story of her own to tell; her manner was so easy to understand that the forthcoming story was inevitable.

"You found the way all right?" asked Cecy, expectantly.

"After a fashion, yes," replied Rosie. "But I had the most hectic time about ten miles from here. I got on the wrong road surely a dozen times, but I managed to find that out, with the help of various kindly disposed filling station men, before I had gotten too far lost. But about ten miles from here I was held up!"

"Held up—not really!" gasped the three girls as one.

"Yes, but I don't mean what you mean. It seems there is some sort of a farm strike going on. A lot of men with guns and sticks were stretched across the road and one of them—a very good-looking young fellow, and very polite, I must say—he had marvelous white teeth and such a tan——"

"Oh, do get on with it!" murmured Cecy. "We know he was swell."

"That's just what he told me to do, to get on, after he had looked in my car and found I didn't have any," laughed Rosie.

"Any what?" asked Carol.

"Any milk, of course."

"Milk!" cried Thally. "Well, for the love of babies! Why milk?"

"That's what I asked him," said Rosie, demurely; she loved this. "And he told me about it. It seems there is a strike among the dairy workers. They weren't letting any milk pass out of a certain district and there had been smuggling of it by some who wouldn't give in to the strikers. As if I would smuggle milk. I just laughed at the good-looker and he laughed back at me."

"A coupla laughers," mocked Thally.

"He really had a very nice smile. And so——"

"So you moved on!" prompted Cecy.

"Yes. He told me a short cut to take and taking it, here I am. La! La! La! Isn't it a lovely day. But you look all hot and bothered. What's doing, my friends? Let your little camp-mate in on it. This is a spooky sort of place, isn't it?"

"You shall hear about that soon, Rosie," promised Carol. "But come in and freshen up. We're all settled, but we didn't know just when you'd arrive."

"Oh, I wouldn't pass this up for anything. I got your note when I returned from a little trip and I packed at once," Rosie told them.

"That was the very thing to do," agreed Carol.

"Though I must say," declared Rosie, referring again to her adventures on the trip, "as a guide map your note was more like directions for playing a fortune-hunting game than anything else."

"Oh, well, you're here!" laughed Cecy, "so it must have been pretty good."

"I'll say I am here. And what a lovely old place! Such a marvelous view, such a quaint old house. I had a glimpse of an ancient mill—I'm going to photograph it—I have my camera. And if here isn't my old friend Rachel!" She hurried across the room to shake hands with the pleased housekeeper. Rosie was one of Rachel's favorite characters.

"Glad you could join us, Rosie," said Rachel demurely. "And what about lunch, Carol-love?" she asked next.

While Carol was giving directions, the other three girls talked rapidly, covering much ground and when Carol was again ready to join in, Rachel having gone back to the kitchen, she heard Rosie say to the girls:

"And now what about the mystery? Isn't this the most lovely and romantic place for a mystery? That old iron scare crow in the hall can do tricks if I'm any judge of character."

"Who mentioned mystery?" asked Carol, wondering how best to put the matter before the new arrival without scaring her away.

"There wasn't any need to mention it," laughed Rosie. "I can see it sticking out all over each one of you. And when, so early in the morning, you come out to greet me, and your hair is all awry and

I see cobwebs on Cecy's elbow and a smudge of
dust on the immaculate Carol—why it just spells
mystery with capital letters. You have been hunt-
ing in dark corners. Come on—tell it to me. I'm
ready!"

She flopped into an easy chair and stuck her feet
out until the pretty pumps almost fell off.

"But honestly, girls, you do look unnaturally
serious over this," Rosie said, she herself at the
moment being unnaturally serious for Rosie.

"Well, there is no use in denying there is—*something,* really—well, weird around this place," admitted Carol in even tones. "We have been listening and waiting not exactly cowardly enough to
run away you know," she sort of apologized. "We
didn't want to mention it in the note to you. It
seems no one can live in this place for very long
and it is very important for Aunt Isabel to either
live here herself or rent the place profitably in
order to retain possession of it. That part is rather
complicated and for lawyers to solve, but the fact
is, Rosie, there are strange noises in this house, up
to now noises only, however."

"But not *just* noises, it's more like—like a fury,"
broke in Cecy. "They are weird—ghostly—haunting groans, moans——"

"And they are calling the old place Moaning
Cliff," broke in Thally. "So it looks as if it is no
mere accident, this noise business."

"How romantic!" bubbled Rosie and a pump did

fall off with her fluttering. "Well, it will take more than moans to spoil my appetite and I'm warning you it's a big one at present. I've had a long ride," she explained. "Moaning Cliff—eh. Sounds like some old Southern Mammy trying to say 'morning.' 'Moanin' t' yo'all, honey! Moanin'!'" She made a comic chant of it and was rewarded with a laugh.

"No, but seriously," said Carol a little later, as they went out to lunch, "we heard them last night. And you may hear them tonight, Rosie, but the boys, Glenn and Ted, are coming tonight so we will need a demonstration."

"More company? Glenn and Ted——"

"You knew how to time your visit, Rosie," teased Cecy, "but go easy on Ted——"

"Oh, grand. Make them stay late," she begged. "I haven't had a good long talk with a young man since——"

"Since the milk hold-up a few hours ago!" mocked Thally.

"Oh, well, I didn't get to know him and I do know Glenn. And I want to meet the Ted. Oh, isn't life wonderful"—and so she rattled on. But the other girls were glad of the merriment. The occurrence of the previous night had been like a shadow hanging over them, and now Rosie was doing a lot to cheer them up.

Glenn and Ted arrived shortly after the evening meal, explained that they had time off until the next morning.   That this meant getting up around 5 o'clock to be back with their camp charges in time for breakfast did not matter to the two youths, it was so good to have a night away from camp routine and restrictions.

It didn't take the girls long to go at their own troubles now that the boys were there to protect them.   Neither did they make any pretense of denying their fears, as they had been doing.   All three chimed in to declare not even one spook but a flock of them must be responsible for the awful disturbances.

"You are not really serious?" questioned Ted. He was tall, light, "good-looking like a poet," Rosie declared later.

"Of course we are serious over this," declared Thally.

"Not serious about believing it's a ghost," contradicted Carol.   "But we do know it's something awful.   We bolt all the doors, and we have had the caretaker and his wife over one night.   Another night, the first, I didn't tell the girls, but Rachel and I had our own *private* scare," she admitted.

"You did!" charged Cecy.

"But never mind that now.   Let's get our great big strong men's opinions.   What do *you* think, Glenn?"

"Wind blowing through some holes in the cellar foundation," said Glenn, as if that settled it.

"Come along then, prove it. Help us find the holes," demanded Cecy.

"Sure," agreed Glenn, readily. "Get the lights."

They searched around, but found nothing to base any real theories upon.

"Could it be some peculiar form of wireless?" asked Carol. "Cecy has a theory that a bed spring or water pipe might pick up broadcasting from a distance. What do you think, boys?"

"Where's your possible method of stepping up the wireless sounds that do undoubtedly reach here from all over as they reach every other place?" asked Glenn. "You've got to have some sort of an electrically energized receiver—tubes, a loud speaker and a lot of traps."

"Nothing like that to be seen around here," Ted chimed in. He had been looking around very carefully. And now they all hurried up stairs.

Settled down again to talk it all over, the girls were more and more insistent that now something must be done.

"Wouldn't the incandescent bulbs act as radio tubes under certain circumstances?" asked Cecy, who seemed determined to put her theory over. "And couldn't water pipes or even the outside electric wires act as an aerial?"

Glenn shook his head in doubt and Ted agreed with him that there was nothing around that could explain the strange noises.

"Of course I'd like to hear the noises before I pass final judgment," said Glenn as seriously as though he might be an expert called in consultation on this matter.

"Stay tonight and listen," begged Thally. "In fact, we are so scared you had *better* stay."

"Do you guarantee we shall have a demonstration?" asked Ted with his nice, wide smile.

"You never can tell," replied Carol. "There really isn't any guarantee."

"Well, I hope we don't have our trip for nothing," remarked Glenn, biting half a cake at once, and making a funny face.

"Well, I like that!" scoffed Cecy. "Don't *we* count?"

"As ghosts, hardly, but there are other considerations," Glenn said, slyly.

CHAPTER XI

NIGHT TERROR

SEEMINGLY they all awakened at once. The two boys were in a room they had insisted on sharing together.

"We fellows got to stick together," Ted had insisted. "The ghostie might have a special hatred of men."

Something had happened. They had been literally shocked awake.

"By golly!" exclaimed Glenn to his chum, "did you hear that?"

"I sure did! What was it—locomotive whistle?"

"We're too far from a railroad here for it to be that."

"But what was it?"

"Search me. Listen!"

They did not want to move. They must listen in perfect silence.

Again that weird scream—a shrill cry of helpless terror.

"That isn't in this house," declared Glenn, moving to get up.

113

"What difference does that make?" demanded Ted. "It's a cry of terror."

"But it may mean that all the girls' noises are outside the house, not inside," Glenn pointed out. "Now, if the noise is outside it may explain something."

"Right as ever, Glenn, old scout. But let's get busy."

"Listen!" warned Glenn again, as this time there reached them noises unmistakably coming from *within* the house. But these were different sounds, not such noises as the two terrified screams that had first sounded to awaken everybody. It was like the pattering of feet to and fro in the hall and certainly those were the voices of the girls and Rachel.

"Oh, what is it?" called Rosie, her door opened a crack. Cecy too was cautiously poking her head out.

Then Thally's vigorous voice questioned: "Is anybody sick?"

"Sick with fear, I guess," Rosie said, her own voice quaking. She never was as brave or as bold as were the other girls, though very merry and light-hearted even in times of trouble. But this was different. It was terror in the night.

"Did you all hear it?" asked Carol.

"As if we could help it!" gasped Cecy. "Oh, what was it? Are the boys up?"

As if in answer to her terrified question came the almost unearthly scream again.

"Call the boys!" urged Rosie. "Quick! Carol! Oh!"

"We're here! Right here!" Glenn assured them as he and Ted barefooted and trailing borrowed bathrobes came pattering down the hall.

"What is it?" asked Ted quite calmly, as boys always do in emergencies.

"If we knew we wouldn't be so excited," Carol answered, trying to laugh but not succeeding very well. "Where does the noise seem to come from, Glenn?"

"Not inside this house, I'm sure of that."

"I thought the same. But——"

Once more the scream of terror and then sudden loud and unmistakable thumps on the front door.

"Oh!" screamed Rosie grasping Cecy at the same moment that Cecy was making a grab at her.

"Some one is trying to get in!" called Thally.

"Don't let them in!" begged Cecy.

"It must be somebody who wants help—who is afraid—of what is happening outside—in the dark," murmured Carol. "We must——"

She was interrupted by more loud thumps. And then a voice, an unmistakable human voice, and with an accent that they all recognized, pleaded:

"Lemme in! Oh, lemme in! Fo' de lub of mammy lemme in!"

More frantic poundings.

"It's a Negro!" said Glenn. "Wait!" he called out loudly.

"Sounds like a boy," reasoned Ted. "And he sure is scared of something."

"Oh, go to him! Go to him!" ordered Carol. "The little fellow may be hurt!"

"If he isn't he's almost scared to death," announced Glenn. "Come on, Ted!"

"Here!" said Carol, passing him her flashlight.

"Oh, all right," Glenn said with a too well marked indifference. "Now don't be alarmed," he reassured them. "It's probably nothing but some boys playing tricks. They do things like that over at camp."

"But not as late as this," Ted reminded him, as he glanced at a hall clock. It was past midnight.

"No, not as late as this," Glenn had to admit.

The two boys hurried down the stairs, the girls and the housekeeper, their first unreasoning terror over, clustered in the hall above, looking down and awaiting developments. As Glenn and Ted went to the door they could still hear thumps and knocks and a small voice calling:

"Lemme in! Lemme in! It done mos' got me! Suah will de nex' time! Oh, golly! I's so scairt! Please lemme in!"

"Poor kid!" murmured Ted. "He is scared."

"Keep quiet!" ordered Glenn as he fumbled with the rusty key in the lock of the big door. "We'll let you in. But do stop howling."

The poundings and the frightened pleas ceased suddenly. And when the door was opened there tumbled, rather than stepped into the hall, a little heap of animated rags, and in the bundle they soon made out a colored boy about twelve years old. He was shaking pitifully with fright, and his lips trembled until bits of saliva dribbled from them. He tried to reach Glenn but collapsed and again fell in a heap on the floor.

"Oh, is he hurt!" cried Carol, starting down the stairs.

"No, just scared," said Glenn, taking a hasty survey. "Now, who are you and what's the matter?" he asked, shaking the boy by a shoulder and speaking sternly in order to check the tremors of terror which were still shaking the little figure. "Snap out of it and tell us!"

"Yes, suh, I—I will. I—I—seen it—it come right at me!"

"What?" demanded Ted.

"De ghos'—de hant—mammy tole me not t' come dis-a-way but I done come, an'—an'——"

"Nonsense! There aren't any ghosts!" said Glenn, shaking the boy again. "Snap out of it, I tell you, and let's hear about it. If you don't I'll put you outside again and——"

"Oh, no! No, doan't do dat! Doan't put me out. I—I'll tell yo'!" the boy pleaded.

"Poor kid!" Thally sympathized, "he's just scared to death."

"Give him a drink of water!" urged Carol. She had hurried back to the bathroom and now came down stairs with a glass of water.

"That may help," Glenn said a trifle grimly. The boy's teeth chattered on the rim of the glass as he gobbled the water, but he managed to gulp it down and then seemed a little calmer. He could not choke and shiver at the same time.

"Now go on, tell us about it," ordered Glenn.

"Yes, suh, I will!" His eyes, big with terror, roved around, seeming to pick out each of the girls who stood about him curiously. "I was goin' fo' de doctor," he began.

"Doctor?" sharply questioned Carol.

"Yes'm. My pappy was tuk sick in de night an' mammy says fo' me t' go fo' de doctor. So I went."

"Where do you live?" asked Glenn.

"On de back road by de ole mill," was the answer. "Pappy used t' wuk in de mill, he tole me, when he was a kid. So, I was goin' fo' de doctor an' it was shorter t' come dis-a-way, by de ole house, but my mammy said fo' me not t' do it."

"Why did she tell you that?" Glenn wanted to know.

"'Count ob de hant."

"What hant? I suppose you mean ghost?" Glenn had assumed the rôle of examiner.

"Yes, suh, dat's it—de ghost. Ev'ybody knows dis ole house, she is hanted. Dey's queer noises an' queer sights." He could roll those eyes like big agates.

The girls were agreeing in glances and gestures that *they* understood these suspicions.

"I didn't ought done t' pass here by night, 'specially 'round de middle ob de night," went on the boy in lamentation.

"Did you get past?" asked Glenn.

"No, suh, I done didn't. I oughter done what mammy said. But pappy had de misery so bad an' mammy said hurry fo' de doctor man, so I hurried de sho't way an' it mos' got me." His bare, black feet had a lot of trouble keeping under his ragged little form. They were all but doubling up.

"But what—what was it?" demanded Glenn.

"De big white hant. It come across de meadow at me, hollerin' an' wavin' its arms an' den I yelled an' rushed heah. I knowed folks had moved in heah, even if my mammy said dey wouldn't stay."

"Why won't we stay?" pressed Carol.

" 'Count ob de hant—de noises an' de awful sights. I seed it—plain, I seed it. Come right at me, it did, an' I run heah an' I pounded on de do'."

"And you yelled, didn't you?" said Ted.

"Suah, I yelled. But de hant—he yelled first, like laffin at me," he tried to explain.

This was significant. It left a question for the mystery investigators to answer. Something or somebody had "yelled" first.

Was it the cries of the colored boy that had aroused them or the noise made by the "ghost?" That was what they should find out.

"Well, you're all right now, boy," said Glenn, soothingly. "Nothing got you, and I think maybe you dreamed you saw the hant."

"No, suh, I didn't dream. I were too skairt t' dream. 'Sides, I want t' git de doctor man fer pappy—he's got de misery pow'ful bad. And now maybe—he's—daid!"

"Was it when you were going for the doctor or coming back that you think you saw this ghost?" asked Carol.

"I suah seen it, missie. An' I hain't been fo' de doctor yit! I was goin' but I dassn't go now. An' pappy'll sho' die ob de misery," he moaned.

"We'll get the doctor for you," offered Glenn. "Don't worry. But now tell us exactly what happened? Can you? *We* need to know."

Though he was calmer, the boy's story did not vary from his first breathless recital. He managed to say he had been crossing the fields back of the old house, to take a short cut to the village, when "suffin big an' white an' screamin'" had rushed at him. He fled in terror, adding his screams and cries for mercy to those of the strange thing, and "knowin' it done had me" he then ran for the house and had frantically pounded on the door of the house. Even then, he insisted, "it kep' a-hantin'."

"Well, I guess that's all we can get out of him," Ted summed up. "Now, what's next?" Ted talked like a time table.

"Oh, if you boys wouldn't mind—you have your car—you could take him to get the doctor," suggested Carol. "Our telephone isn't working yet. But I'm determined to get the man over the first thing in the morning to have it connected; we need it," she added significantly.

"They are useful," admitted Glenn. "Come on, Ted, we'll finish the job."

The boys went to dress while the girls talked further with the frightened little colored boy.

"What's your name?" asked Carol, kindly.

"Toledo, missie. Toledo Jackson."

"Toledo!" murmured Carol, with a smiling glance at the others. "Why, that's the name of a city."

"I knows it, yes'm, missie. My pappy wuked dere once, an' he liked de place so he named me fo' it. I'se Toledo Jackson."

"Well, Toledo, you won't be afraid any more," soothed Cecy. "You'll have two good protectors you know, men who will take care of you, and they'll see that the doctor gets to your father as soon as he can."

Glenn and Ted came hurrying down stairs.

"Come on, kid!" invited Glenn, without any more nonsense.

"You won't be away any longer than you can help, will you?" asked Rosie. She had something like the colored boy's shakes, it seemed.

"Why?" asked Ted, winking at his chum.

"Oh, I just thought——"

"Say, listen," said Glenn, as Toledo Jackson followed Ted outside, "this kid just imagined things. What he probably saw was a white cow."

"Do cows yell?" asked Ted.

"That was just his imagination. It was probably the echoes of his own yells he heard. Forget it!"

The girls did their best to take a sane view of the incident, but they did not go back to bed until the sound of the boys' auto was heard returning. They had persuaded a doctor to go to Toledo's father, but not easily, for he seemed to be too familiar with the case.

"So that's that," remarked Glenn. "And now again how about bed."

"Hardly worth while," yawned Ted. "We've got to get up so early."

"What time?" Carol asked.

"We're going to hit the trail back to camp about five, if we can," Glenn answered.

"Why so early?" continued Cecy.

"Duty calls. But we'll see you again. Nighty-night!" and this time it was made unanimous.

CHAPTER XII

THE VOICE OF THE WHEEL

THE boys arose at the hour they had set for themselves, and not one of the girls heard them go, so soundly did they sleep after that night terror which yet remained to be explained.

Rachel, however, faithful Rachel, was "on the job" and was up even before Glenn and Ted, having orange juice and steaming coffee ready for them, for the early dawn was cold.

"You shouldn't have bothered!" objected Glenn in thanking her.

"It is no bother. Besides, we all want you to come again," insisted Rachel.

"You mean—because of—of what may yet happen? That there is danger here?" asked Ted.

"Yes—at least for what the girls think may happen. As for me—I don't believe a word of it— just stray dogs!" asserted the housekeeper, defiantly.

"It might have been dogs at that," admitted Glenn as they took their leave.

When the girls came down they were sorry to

123

have missed the boys, and of course, they started right in to talk of the night's happenings.

"This place hasn't a very savory reputation, it seems," remarked Rosie, sarcastically, toying with her buttered toast.

"Are you sorry you came?" asked Cecy in surprise.

"Not at all! I love ghosts and mysteries and hants—especially when Carol has guaranteed to settle their hash."

"Oh, I didn't do anything of the kind!" protested Carol.

"Well, you will, I feel sure of it," laughed the irrepressible Rosie.

So the talk went on. After breakfast the girls spent the morning over their few duties and then went for a swim. In the afternoon they strolled in the cool and shady woods. They were a little nervous as night approached, but Carol, rising to the occasion, made so light of Toledo's visit and what had so far happened, that they were all in a merry mood as they went to bed. One and all agreed that they would not desert while it were possible to stay.

"We promised Aunt Isabel," was Carol's watchword and her friends rallied to her banner.

Rosie was particularly skeptical about there being anything weird or inexplainable about Rocky Ledge.

"Not counting Toledo," she said, "I have yet to be thrilled or scared."

"But we did hear noises," said Thally, and they again told of their excursion to the cellar.

"Well, why didn't you save some for me?"

Three eventless days passed—days filled with happy hours of doing really very little except bathe, go to the village or stroll in the woods or by the mill. Once, on a visit to the town, Carol thought she heard some one of a group of idlers near the drugstore say:

"Them's the ones that live in Moaning Cliff."

"Yeah? Well, you wouldn't get me to live there —nor pass it at night."

"Bunk!"

"I tell you it ain't bunk!"

Carol hurried on, glad that none of the others had heard.

The fourth day after the Toledo visit had passed as pleasantly as the other three. In the morning the girls had gone in for their usual bathing relaxation. In the early afternoon some girls from Melody Lane, motoring through Cedarshore, and knowing Carol and her friends were at Rocky Ledge, had stopped in for a little visit. It made a welcome, if brief break in their routine.

Then, as their guests left, Carol proposed that, as the day was cool, they walk over toward the old mill. The place seemed to fascinate her. They went together, all four girls, with merry laughter, and even snatches of song, until they almost forgot about the suspended dread and anxiety.

Cautiously they crossed the rustic bridge over the stream that once gave power to the old mill. Then Bell Bonner danced in the middle of it to make her wish come true. Carol insisted she would try no tricks as a shaky bridge was nothing to fool with.

The old mill wheel was moving slightly under the influence of a strong wind, and the little water that reached its buckets from the half-chocked flume. Now and then it creaked a little, but to the suggestion of Rosie, that perhaps this creaking might account for the groans, the others turned deaf ears. It couldn't have been that.

A few more uneventful days and then, suddenly in the night, once more the house was filled with the awful moans which this time awakened even the sound-sleeping Rosie. Through the rooms the sounds echoed weirdly, welling up from the cellar it seemed "and trying to get out," as Cecy said.

"Oh—hhh! Ah—hhh! UUmmmmmm!" The groans crescendoed into wails then shrieks, and finally died away in a long, sighing rumble, like the last breath of a dying——

"Oh, what is it? What is it?" Rosie positively wailed as she ran to Carol's room.

"What did we tell you?" demanded Thally. "Now are you satisfied?"

"You never told me it was anything like this!"

snapped the newcomer. "No wonder tenants won't stay here. I—I——"

"We're going to see if we can catch them this time!" said Carol firmly. "Come on, girls!"

With startled eyes they saw her reach for her flashlight as Rachel came pattering along the hall. For the night terror had gripped her also, grim Scotchwoman that she was, and she knew her place was beside her frightened young charges.

Rosie, all her bubbling laughter hushed and the glint of amusement gone from her eyes, clung to Carol in sheer terror.

"Let go of me, Rosie dear," Carol pleaded. "We must find out about this now, while it's— going!"

"You mean this terrible noise? How can you?"

"The moans—yes. We must try to follow them——"

The distracting sounds were still echoing through the house, though not as loudly as first when the noises had been simply ear-splitting.

"What are you going to do?" Obviously Rosie was ready to do an "ostrich act," as Cecy said later, and hide her head beneath a pillow.

"We must discover, if possible, what makes the noises," Carol said fairly. "And to do this we must go where they seem to come from."

"You mean the—the cellar?" Rosie faltered.

"Yes."

"Oh, I'll never go down there!"

"We were down the other night," Thally stated. "But we had the caretaker with us then."

"We can go get Jensen now, if you wish," Carol agreed. "But I thought——"

"You mean we might find out more if *he* wasn't along?" guessed Cecy as her sister hesitated.

"Yes," said Carol, flatly.

"I think so myself," Cecy agreed. "Come on, Rosie, be a sport!"

"There is no danger—none at all!" insisted Rachel. "I'm sure we'll find the dogs this time— ugly brutes destroying a body's sleep!"

She had her flashlight in readiness, and after a little persuasion Rosie agreed to get her light and soon they were again parading toward the cellar.

As the inner door was unlocked a series of wails, so shrill and terrifying came up in one blast that they all stood still, listening in spite of their new fears. Rosie screamed outright, but Cecy pinched her and the scream was changed to a half howl. Finally she too stopped and listened.

It was very dark and quiet as they bravely started down. Then Carol thought of something that had escaped them on the previous visit. She switched on the cellar lights from a knob at the top of the stairs.

"Oh, that's a relief!" sighed Thally. "We didn't know there was a light."

It must be said that Carol's legs trembled a little as she boldly walked down the cellar stairs with

Rachel beside her. Cecy, Thally and Rosie followed cautiously.

Once in the cellar the intense silence following that barrage of moans, groans and shrieks was almost painful to the ears it made so sharp a contrast. They began to search at once. First one area was looked over thoroughly and gradually until the whole place was gone over without the slightest clue being uncovered. The outside cellar door was found to be securely fastened from outside and not a window had been opened or tampered with. Each one was fastened by an inside bolt.

"What do you say, now, Carol?" asked Cecy as they started back for the stairway again.

"What Alice said," was the answer.

"Alice who?" Rosie wanted to know.

"In Wonderland—it is curiousier and curiousier," joked Carol.

"'Tis surely strange!" murmured Rachel. "I would have sworn I'd find dogs." She, at least, seemed disappointed.

"Dogs or cats," said Thally.

"No—dogs." The housekeeper was insisting on her rights. "Cats have a different tone," she explained.

"I'll need something to tone up my nerves if this keeps up!" said Rosie. "I don't see how you girls stand it!"

"This is only the second time," said Cecy.

"That's twice too much!" said Rosie. "Let's get out of here."

"We could send for Glenn again," ventured Cecy. "He said he or Ted would come over any time of the night if we telephoned. We have a phone here and there's one in the camp headquarters—Glenn sleeps there and he told me there was always a man on duty all night. Let's ask him to come over!" she pleaded.

"Oh, do!" begged Rosie.

"No," Carol decided. "He could see no more here than we have seen—which is nothing."

"But he could hear the moans," said Cecy.

"They aren't moaning now," her sister reminded her curtly.

"I should think he'd be glad of the chance to come over while it's working," said Rosie.

"And if he or Ted came," supplemented Cecy, "they could put their ears to those water pipes, and say whether it might not be wireless we are being terrorized with."

"Try it yourself," suggested Carol.

Gingerly Cecy applied her ear to a damp, cold pipe, squealing a little at the shock. But after a moment of listening she shook her head.

"Nothing," she said.

Finally they went up stairs, locking the door after them, still debating about sending for Jensen. Eventually they decided against it. As Carol said, he might only turn cranky if routed out of bed a second time for nothing.

"We'll solve this mystery ourselves," she declared, seeming more courageous and hopeful since nothing in the cellar had jumped out at them.

It was almost morning when the girls again sought their rooms and got back to sleep, each one with flashlight laid where it could be easily reached. But there was no further need.

Day dawned with the usual bright sun and the greeting of the early birds. It was rather a wan and dispirited quartette of girls that gathered about the breakfast table. But Rachel showed no sign of weariness. There was the same cheerful smile on her face as she served the coffee and in answer to a remark by Carol she said, grimly:

"I'll catch 'em yet—the dogs!"

After what might be termed a council of war, the girls decided to drive to Camp Tagawah again and report to Glenn upon events of the night. They found the camp boys playing ball with Ted umpiring. Glenn hurried to them.

"Glad you came," he said, a little surprised. "But you missed the best part of the game," he told them.

"We have something else to think of besides ball games," Cecy remarked with a great show of importance.

"Ghosts again?" asked Glenn.

"Moans—the same thing in another form," spoke Carol.

Glenn whistled. "Ted!" he called, "we've got our work cut out for us now," as Ted was through his game, and now joining the party.

"Sure thing!" agreed Ted.

"Listen, Carol," Glenn went on, "next week we'll have a little more time off—the camp will be pretty nearly running itself then, and we can spend more time at your place. Meanwhile—hold the fort."

"Aye, aye, Captain!" chanted Thally. "But be sure and send reinforcements if we are besieged."

"I shall. How about our coming over tonight?"

"We aren't likely to hear any noises tonight," said Carol. "So far they have never come two nights in succession. Why that is I don't know. But wait about three days and then—we may telephone you."

"We'll be seeing you!" Glenn promised. "As a matter of fact, it would have been a little strain to get over tonight. We have some initiatory ceremonies for the new members of the camp lodge. But if you want us, even late tonight, give us a ring."

"And we'll come running in the faithful old flivver!" Ted promised.

But the night proved to be quiet and the girls were glad of it. Then for three nights nothing happened. All was peaceful in the old mansion.

Late one afternoon Rosie, whose first pictures of the old mill were failures because she forgot, in her excitement, to turn the film spool, again loaded her camera with a fresh supply and started out to try it again. Carol went with her for she wanted to explore the old mill. Cecy and Thally had gone to the village to do some shopping so that Carol and Rosie had the sight-seeing to themselves.

Soon they could hear the water splashing as they neared the old ruins. It was a mere trickle at first, sending forth a cooling sound upon the hot summer air. Then, suddenly, the flow of water was increased. A quick little flood seemed to have been admitted into the flume when it fell down upon the buckets of the ponderous, mossy wheel, thus giving the power of turning it. In its working days the mill would have readily responded to this stimulus of falling water, but now the wheel seemed rusted into place—almost immovable.

But as Rosie poised herself on a jutting rock to make a snapshot, and as Carol went a little farther below her where she could look up at the great wheel and the flume above it, the big circle of wood, now almost hidden beneath moss and weeds, began to turn. It creaked, it groaned, whined and almost moaned!

"Oh," gasped Rosie. "The awful sounds again!"

"No," said Carol. "They are different—just

natural sounds of a creaking wheel. They have nothing to do——"

She ceased suddenly. There was a cry—a cry of anguish:

"Help! Help! Oh, I'm slipping! Where are you, Jessie! Help!"

Horror stricken, Carol and Rosie stood listening. Then, as Rosie dropped her camera she gasped:

"The wheel speaks! It's talking!"

CHAPTER XIII

SANDS OF DEATH

STARTLED and surprised, Rosie and Carol might easily have believed that the voice they heard actually came from within the great mill wheel, which was slowly turning, creaking and groaning. But in another moment, when again the call for help was heard and the appeal rang out for "Jessie," Carol caught more accurately the direction from which the voice came and she exclaimed:

"It's a man! He's down under the wheel! I see him!"

"A man! Where?" gasped Rosie hurrying to where Carol stood.

"There! Down below! On the spillway." She pointed to a sloping platform of wood, below the great wheel. This platform sloped sharply and the boards were slimy with moss and water growths. A thin film of water was flowing over it, coming from the pond above which was held back by a dam that made the water deep enough so it would flow over the buckets of the wheel and so turn it.

Then Rosie saw at what Carol pointed. A young

man was sprawled upon this slimy, slippery spillway, one leg was under him and his whole body
seemed twisted in pain.   His arms were outstretched, and as the girls watched they could see
his fingers vainly trying to get a hold on the smooth,
slippery boards of the spillway, to stop his dangerous sliding.

For he was slipping toward a deep pool of water
below the wheel, and it needed but a glance to show
that if he once plunged in he would not be able to
help himself.   And he seemed, injured, hurt.

"Help me!   Help me!" he gasped as he continued slowly to slide along toward the dangerously
deep pool.   "Where—is—Jessie?"

Carol did not trouble to answer this question,
for she saw the need of instant action.

"Come on, Rosie!" she called.

"Where?"

"Down there!   We must stop him from sliding
into the pool."

"Oh, Carol, I want to help but we can never get
down there!"

"Yes, we can.   We can climb down on these
stones.   They're not slippery.   They're almost like
steps.   Once we are down there we can reach over
and pull him to one side of the spillway.   Then he
won't be in any danger and we can bring help.
Come on!" she hurriedly ordered.

Made brave by Carol's daring move, Rosie, after

but an instant of hesitation, followed. Carol
paused only to call:

"We're coming! We'll get you! Hold on—if
you—can!"

"You—you'll have to hurry!" answered the
young man faintly. "I'm slipping fast, and I can't
get a—hold—on these—slimy—boards."

The stones, which formed the outer face of the
old mill dam were, indeed, almost like a rough
flight of steps. It was not difficult for Rosie and
Carol to make their way down to the level of the
spillway, and their footing was firm, for here the
boards were dry, without any treacherous coating
of slimy moss. In fact, there was even a little sur-
face coating of sand and gravel which made it possible for the girls to brace their feet in readiness
for the strain that would soon be upon them.

Slowly the young man slid nearer and nearer to
what seemed an inevitable plunge into the deep
pool. But he was also sliding in a lateral direction,
toward the two girls. And, just when it seemed as
if he must slide over the edge of the spillway, Carol
and Rosie, stooping down and extending their
hands, grasped the edge of his coat and pulled him
toward them. He slid easily on the slimy boards,
and in the pulling his bent leg was straightened out.
At this a spasm of pain passed over his face, but
he suppressed a groan of anguish and managed
feebly to murmur:

"Thanks—I—I'll be all right now. I can't slip any farther. But I can't get up. I—I'm afraid my leg is broken. If you can find Jessie—she went to get help after I fell—but——"

"We didn't see anyone," said Carol, releasing her hold of the young man's coat, as did Rosie also. They saw that he was in a safe, if not very comfortable, position. "Who is Jessie?"

"She is my sister. Our car is somewhere up there," he motioned to the top of the dam. "I sent her for help when I found I couldn't get back after I fell off the big wheel."

"What were you doing on the mill wheel?" asked Carol.

"Just inspecting it. I'm an engineer and——"

At this moment a voice called from the top of the dam, close to the stone stairway where Rosie and Carol had climbed down. Looking up they saw a young girl.

"I've brought help, Barry!" she cried. "Two men—they'll be here in a moment. I ran on ahead after I found them! Oh, but how did you get over there?" she asked in evident surprise.

"I slid part way, on the slimy planks, and these young ladies were kind enough to pull me over to safety. Otherwise I might now be in the pool," he answered in a shaken voice.

"Oh, Barry! What a terrible accident! And how wonderful that these girls could help you! Are you—are you much hurt?"

"Only my leg. Broken I'm afraid. But it might be a lot worse."

"Of course. Oh, here are the men!" She stepped aside as the forms of two men were seen outlined against the sky on the edge of the dam. Carol recognized one of the men as Emil Jensen. The other was Jed Bailey, the lobsterman. All three girls were too anxious even to speak.

"Well, what's the matter of gettin' him out first an' askin' him how he got there later?" demanded Jed. "Don't worry, young feller," he added, kindly. "We'll soon have you up. You girls had better climb back up here," he went on to Rosie and Carol. "There ain't much leeway down there."

"That's right," agreed Emil.

"Let's climb back, girls," proposed Carol. "We can't do any more. He'll be all right now."

"Oh, I certainly hope so!" Rosie still seemed spellbound.

It was not easy work for the caretaker and lobsterman to carry the injured young man up the crazy flight of mill dam steps, for after a trial, when they had raised him, the youth found he could not bear his weight on his left leg. So he could not help himself. But the two men were sturdy and accustomed to heavy weights, Jed perhaps being the better at this from long years of hauling up his lobster pots from the depths of the sea. Finally, the youth was put in a comfortable position, sitting on the grass with his back against an old apple tree that grew on the edge of the mill pond.

"I—I guess I'll be all right now," he faltered. "Thank you all for what you've done."

"The job ain't done yit!" declared Jed with a grim smile. "You can't walk an' you need a doctor. One of us had better go fetch him."

"If he could be taken to a doctor I think it would be better," proposed the sister. "Barry can't be left here, anyhow, so he might as well be taken to the doctor first."

"I was thinkin' of his leg," said the lobsterman. "If it's broke it ain't wise to move it till it's put in splints. Otherwise the bone's likely to come through, an' that's bad."

"I don't believe, after all, that my leg is broken," said the young man. "But it is badly sprained. Certainly I can't walk on it but I don't believe it will do any harm to move me. If you would be so kind as to carry me to our car, my sister can drive us to where we are staying and the doctor can fix me up there."

"You living here in town?" asked Emil Jensen, rather sharply.

"Not exactly living here," was the answer, given with a somewhat wan smile. "My sister and I are spending our vacation touring about in an auto. My name is Barry Brennan; I live in New York City. We reached here this morning and decided to stay for a few days. We inquired for a boarding place and were directed to a Mrs. Ronnie and we took rooms there."

"You got a good place," commented Jed. "Alvirah Ronnie will feed you good and look after you top notch. She buys her lobsters offen me and they're always the best."

"Well, we haven't been fortunate enough, yet, to have lobster," said Mr. Brennan, smiling again. "But I shall live in hope. After we unpacked at Mrs. Ronnie's, my sister and I started out to explore. We drove past this old mill and it attracted me. While Jessie was gathering some flowers in the fields I started to investigate the big wheel. I wanted to see how it was geared to the shaft that must have operated the mill stones in the days when this place was working. Unfortunately, I did not allow for the slippery, slimy condition of the wheel. I climbed out on it. Unexpectedly it began to turn. I slipped and fell to the spillway, my leg getting twisted under me."

"I heard him call for help," said Jessie Brennan taking up the story for her brother seemed exhausted. "But I saw I could not do anything by myself so I ran for help."

"And then I felt myself slipping along the spillway toward the pool," went on Mr. Brennan. "I realized I could not help myself if I plunged in, so I began to call again. And then these young ladies came along and—well, they just about saved me." He smiled at Carol and Rosie gratefully, as did

Jessie, also. He was still suffering and looked it.

"I'm glad we could help," said Carol. "Perhaps you weren't in as much danger as you thought."

"Oh, yes I was. And I don't mind admitting I was pretty well scared. But I'm all right now. And if you gentlemen can carry me to my car, my sister will drive me to Mrs. Ronnie's and we'll see what the doctor says about the old leg."

"We'll do it," said Jed, "and as easy as we can." Jed was kind and not ashamed to show it.

Carol and Rosie walked with Jessie back to the young engineer's car which was parked in the road not far from the path that led to the mill pond. On the way Jessie Brennan related how she had run to the Jensen cottage. She said she had found the caretaker there just concluding a deal for some lobsters with Jed so the two men hurried to the rescue.

"I hope you will come to see us," Jessie invited, as she took her place behind the steering wheel after her brother had been carefully placed in the seat beside her.

"I shall want to thank you more fully than I've had a chance to now," added Mr. Brennan. "Please come." He was almost as nice as Glenn, Rosie thought.

"We shall," promised Carol as the injured man was driven away.

"Well, Cedarshore is gettin' to be a right lively place," commented Jed as he stood beside Emil.

"What with New York folks comin' to board at Alvirah's and you city girls comin' to live at the old place— Are you still there?" he shot at Carol.

"Of course. Why not?" she asked.

"Oh, well, considerin' the reputation of the place, ghosts and queer noises an' all that——"

"Bosh!" interrupted Emil. "I never heard no noises there."

"We have!" declared Rosie, and she gave a little shiver to prove it.

"But we don't in the least mind them!" said Carol, quickly, as if testing Jensen's motives.

"You don't?" It was a sharp question from the caretaker.

"Not at all. In fact we rather enjoy them," declared Carol. "And before we leave we are going to find out what causes them." This was a direct challenge.

"Um!" It was a mumble from Mr. Jensen which might mean almost anything.

"Well, different folks have different likes," said Jed, philosophically. "Some folks won't eat lobster. But there's talk in town," he added, "about that colored boy—Toledo—seein' a ghost out your way. How about it?" he asked Carol.

"Oh, the poor boy was scared, in the middle of the night, by a white cow running at him as he was crossing the lot to get the doctor for his sick father," said Carol simply.

"Hum," murmured the lobsterman. "Ain't nobody around here got a white cow; have they, Emil?"

"How should I know? I got to get back to my chores," and Emil Jensen, "old sour-face," as Cecy described him, turned away.

"Queer chap, that Emil," commented Jed, as he looked at the girls, a quizzical smile on his bronzed face. "Don't you find him so?"

"Really we don't know much about him," said Carol, rather coldly.

The caretaker was soon out of sight amid the trees, and the girls turned back to get the camera Rosie had dropped, as Jed departed to his lobster-pots.

"What made you say that, Carol?" asked Rosie as, with the recovered camera, they were on their way back to the house.

"Say what?"

"About us not minding the ghost noises? You know we *do* mind them."

"Oh, I wasn't going to let Jensen know that we did. It's part of my plan to get at the bottom of this mystery. Once admit we are terribly frightened worse things may happen, and whoever is to blame may trick us further."

"Oh, I hope not. Well, we'll stick with you, Carol," declared Rosie. "Wasn't this an exciting adventure?"

"Somewhat." Carol had to be indifferent to hide her own feelings.

"Cecy and Thally will be wild when they hear what they missed."

Cecy and Thally weren't exactly wild, but they were much interested in hearing about the young engineer and his sister, and they had to be told all the details down to the color of his eyes and hair.

That afternoon they all drove to the home of Mrs. Alvirah Ronnie, in the village, to inquire about the injured man. His sister met the girls and, stating that her brother was now asleep after the doctor's visit, said that the leg was not broken but so badly strained and wrenched that it would mean an enforced stay in bed for some time.

"Oh, that's too bad!" said Carol, sincerely.

"It might be worse," said Jessie Brennan. "At least we have a lovely place to stay. I never saw such a view as that from the top of your cliff. I think it is yours—where the big house stands?" she said. "I was up there for a moment."

"Yes, we are at Rocky Cliff," said Carol. "Do come and see us!"

"I shall. Thank you. And now I must get back to Barry. He is so grateful to you," and she nodded at Carol and Rosie. "He will be sure to want to see you—later."

"Oh, it wasn't anything," Carol said. "But it was lucky we happened to be near."

The call had served to make the girls better acquainted, and the interest thus begun seemed promising for further friendship.

It might have been expected that an exciting night would have followed the exciting day, but it did not. As a matter of fact, not a groan or a moan resounded through the old house and, as Rosie said at breakfast: "A peaceful sleep was had by all."

Next day Rosie and Carol again called to inquire about the young engineer. His sister, Jessie, insisted that they come to her brother's room and let him thank them, which they did. Barry Brennan was profuse in gratefulness. As they came away he said:

"I'm not going to let that old wheel get the best of me. I'm going to find out how it operates as soon as I can get around again."

"Barry!" his sister exclaimed, "if you climb up there again——"

"When I do I'll put on spiked football shoes so I won't slip," he promised with a smile.

It was late afternoon when Rosie and Carol went back, and Rosie asked to be let out of the car near where a path led down to the beach at the foot of the cliff.

"I want to go sit down on the sand and paddle my feet in the water," she said. "I just feel like doing something silly."

"All right," Carol agreed. "But don't be too long, and take care of yourself," she cautioned. "I must see Rachel about dinner."

Left to herself, Rosie wandered about the sands,

admired the calm and distant blue sea, watched the gulls wheeling over the bay and finally, taking off her shoes and stockings, began to wade in the little splashing waves. The tide was slowly coming in. A stretch of yellow sand attracted the girl and she walked toward it, noting that a little stream flowed through it, shimmering in the slowly sinking sun.

"How lovely and soft this sand is," thought Rosie as she stopped upon it. Her bare feet sank in as though being immersed in feathers. "Just wonderful! The other sand is so sharp and coarse."

She took perhaps half a dozen steps away from the edge of yellow sand, where there was a sharp line of demarcation between that and the whiter variety. Her feet sank in deeper and deeper!

"How it clings," she was thinking. "It's like some sticky——"

A strange fear came over her. She had noticed the increasing difficulty in pulling her feet out each time she took a step. And now, suddenly, she was unable to free herself, to move at all!

"Oh!" she gasped. "Oh, I'm caught! I'm caught!"

Deeper and deeper her feet sank into the treacherous quicksand, and the sudden panic she felt come over her seemed to choke her attempt at calling for help.

CHAPTER XIV

THUMPS AND BUMPS

Rosie's heart was beating so hard that it seemed almost to stop her breath. In a moment she was in a wild panic of fear, as she felt herself sinking deeper and deeper and realized that she could not free her feet and legs from that soft but tenacious grip of the clinging sand. She now could scarcely move at all.

"But I must get out! I must pull myself loose!" she heard herself saying in gasps. "I can't die this way!"

She leaned her weight first on one foot and then on the other, following each effort with a desperate attempt to pull herself free. But she only sank the deeper. Then, there rushed into her mind all the terrorizing stories she had read about those engulfed in the quicksands—how they gradually sank deeper and deeper, how the mingled sand and water came up first to the hips, then to the chest, then to the neck and finally, with horrible slowness, to the lips; and that was the end! Even in her frenzied state she recalled reading about some victims who, in their struggles, had fallen forward or back and

148

then, unable to rise, had died more quickly as the body was more easily coerced in a prone position than when erect. Why did these thoughts come now to terrify her?

"I mustn't do that! I mustn't do that!" sobbed Rosie. "I must stand still—I can keep the sand away from my face longer, then. I mustn't fall! No! No!"

She ceased to struggle, ceased trying to pull her feet loose. But then, when she found that she was still slowly sinking she gave way to the panic of terror again and cried:

"Help! Oh, help! Help—me!"

She put all her energies into that wild appeal for help. She heard her voice echo back from the frowning cliff on the summit of which was perched the weird old house of noises. And then came back, not another echo but a welcome and reassuring shout of:

"Steady! I'm coming for you! Steady! Don't fight any more or you'll only go deeper. Steady!"

Rosie turned enough to look and see running toward her Jed Bailey, the old lobsterman. Over his arm was a bundle of tarred fish nets. He was running fast across the firm, white sand.

"Don't be scared!" he shouted. "I'm comin' to you! I'll have you out in a moment. But keep still!" He fairly yelled these last words, and Rosie had sense enough to obey. Then, though she trembled, she watched more calmly the quick and efficient manner in which Jed came to her rescue. What a blessed relief to see him coming!

He ran to the edge of the little, trickling stream but stopped short when he reached the place where the wavering line divided the yellow sand from the white. There he tossed in front of him the matted mass of net. It served as does a plank upon thin ice, and thus the lobsterman was able to cross safely until cautiously he stood beside Rosie. The clinging sand was now up to her knees.

"Now do as I say," ordered Jed sharply, when he had kicked the loose mass of the net close to the frightened girl. "Lean over toward me and put your arms around my neck. Don't be bashful, I'm old enough to be your grandfather," and he laughed even then.

Rosie too laughed, although rather hysterically.

"All right!" she gasped. "But do you—do you think you can get me loose?" She felt as if held in leaden molds.

"Of course I can! You won't be the first I've rescued from Cliff Sands—that's what we call 'em around here—nasty, treacherous sands they are, too! Why did you venture on 'em? Didn't anybody tell you to keep away?"

"No. I've only been here a little while."

"Oh, my! They should have told you. I warned 'em proper!"

"They probably meant to tell me but forgot—

so much has happened since Carol came here to—well, really, I don't know why she came or why I came—I wish I hadn't!" Rosie was on the verge of tears again.

"Tut! Tut! Don't worry. Everything is going to be all right. As for things happening—they have been for quite some spell at Moaning Cliff—but nobody got hurt. Now you aren't going to be hurt, either. Lean over and grab me around the neck! Quick! We haven't any time to lose. This sand works quick!"

Rosie did as she was told, and got a firm clasp of Jed's bronzed and wrinkled neck. He put his arms around her hips as he stooped down. And then, supported as he was by the fishnet, he gave a pull, a jerk and a mighty heave and Rosie was free of the clinging sands. Then Jed straightened up, still holding Rosie, "for all the world like a bag of meal over his shoulder," she told the girls later.

He set her down upon the net, against which the treacherous quicksands pulled in vain. They were both standing upon it now, safe from further harm.

"There!" exclaimed the lobsterman as he straightened up. "Now run across the net to the white sand—that's safe. I'll follow you. And you're all right!" He chuckled loudly.

"Oh, yes, I know I'm all right now!" half sobbed Rosie. "But I was terribly frightened! Terribly!" she panted. It had been dreadful to think of death.

"You have a right to be. They had a right to warn you. After this, keep away from Cliff Sands," reiterated Jed.

"I shall! Oh, and thank you, ever, ever so much!"

"Oh, bosh! 'Twan't nothin'! You'd do the same for me." Jed followed her across his safety net to the firm sands and then pulled the meshes toward him, bundling it in his brawny, brown arms. "'Twas lucky I come along when I did," he remarked reflectively.

"Indeed it was. I shall never forget it," said Rosie solemnly.

"Where's your shoes?" he asked. He, himself, wore rubber boots.

"Over there." She pointed.

"Well, better get 'em on and head for home—if you call that home up there." He nodded toward the house on the frowning cliff.

"It isn't my home," said Rosie, "but we girls are staying there."

"Until the ghost, or whatever it is, drives you out same as it has the others," he said, with that laugh that was a part of his own good nature.

"I think Carol will take some driving," Rosie said. "She's a fighter."

"Carol? Hum! She's the masterful one, ain't she?" he asked.

Realizing that this perfectly described Carol,

Rosie said: "Yes. She is determined to solve the mystery, too."

"Well, it's a mystery all right. Ain't no getting away from that. But don't worry. You can always move out." He chuckled again and went on to his boat with his clean-smelling, tarred net, and Rosie felt she had found a real friend in old Jed.

She washed her feet in the little waves of the bay, keeping close to the edge in the firm, white sands. She dried them with the warm, South wind and then, slipping on her stockings and shoes, she climbed up the cliff path to the house.

"Wherever have you been?" asked Carol as Rosie reached the porch.

"Caught in the quicksands," said Rosie tragically. "The lobsterman pulled me out."

"The quicksands— Oh!" cried Carol, fear and contrition in her voice. "How terrible! I meant to warn you, Rosie. I'll never forgive myself! How awful! Oh, you poor child. However did it slip my mind!" She was gazing at Rosie in real anguish.

"It's all right," said Rosie. "You have a lot on your mind besides quicksands. I should have been more careful when I saw the difference in the color of the sand. But I'll keep away from now on, you can bet on that."

"Oh, Rosie!" Carol continued to lament, as if the thought of her young friend's danger was still unbearable. But youthful spirits are hard to keep down and soon they were listening to Rosie's account of what, after all, might have been a tragic adventure. Great praise was given to Jed for his promptness and for his clever handling of the situation; everyone cheered for Jed.

"After this I'm going to hang a piece of fishnet in my room as a sort of shrine," declared Rosie, "and a warning too."

They sat up rather late that night in Rocky Cliff, for there was a tense, nervous feeling over all of them following Rosie's escape. Rachel had been in her own room several hours when the girls finally came up stairs, Carol and Thally having gone all over the lower floors to see that doors and windows were locked. They had looked last at the inside door leading down into the cellar, having previously gone out, with flashlights, to make certain the outer one was made secure. So now in their own rooms they knew that they had taken no chances.

Then, unexpected, unheralded and like a clap of thunder the terror came again.

It sounded in the stillness of the night. It awakened them all. First, as if from the very depths of the earth, came deep moans, and then shriller cries and then a new manifestation.

For the whole of the great, old house seemed to tremble under the impulse of thumps and bumps. It was as though a giant were smiting the walls with a sledge hammer. The walls vibrated and pictures on them clattered their frames against the plaster.

"Carol!   Carol!" came a cry from Cecy. "What is it!"

A rattling and banging drowned her voice.

"That Chinese warrior is coming up stairs!" shouted Thally as she threw open her door. "Oh, Carol, why didn't we shut him up in the closet as we planned?   It must be———"

"Do something!" begged Cecy.   "Telephone Jensen!" With the installation of a regular line telephone, there had also been added to the old house a branch line to the cottage of the caretaker.

"Just a moment!" begged Carol who, almost in as much of a panic as were her companions, was trying to locate her flashlight beneath her pillow. She switched it on and went out into the hall, not delaying for slippers or robe. She saw the forms of Cecy and Thally emerge from their room.

There was no sign of Rosie.

Could she not have heard the terrorizing noises —the thumps, bumps and groans?

CHAPTER XV

THE SWOOPING GHOST

ALMOST at the same moment the identical idea occurred to Cecy and Thally. They, too, had noticed that Rosie had not rushed out to find the cause of the strange noises still continuing, though now they were not so loud.

"Where is Rosie?" Cecy asked. "Has she———"

Again there resounded another terrifying sound. It was not a moan this time—it was a shriek—shrill and high.

"Oh, this is awful!" gasped Thally. "We must get Jensen here—or somebody. I can't stand it. Carol, what can we do?"

"We must first see if Rosie is all right," decided Carol as calmly as she could. But in spite of her efforts her voice had a tremble in it, just as there were tremors in her legs and in the hand that held the flashlight. "Come," she went on, "we must look in her room."

Once more a blessed silence spread itself through the old house and in this silence, with Carol in the lead and Cecy and Thally holding hands as they walked together, they advanced to Rosie's door.

It opened. Lights flashed within—flashed upon the tumbled, disordered bed but not upon the form of the girl who should have been lying there.

This fact seemed to smite the three girls as though they had been dealt a heavy blow. Their hearts pounded madly.

"She—she isn't here!" whispered Cecy.

"Some one must have come up here and taken her," breathed Thally.

Carol did not speak. She acted. She strode across the room and pulled open a closet door.

There cowering back among her clothes hanging from the hooks, with her hands pressed over her ears and her eyes tightly shut, crouched Rosie. Carol reached out and pulled Rosie's hands down from her face.

"Silly girl!" she chided, trying to put some laughter into her voice with her relief. "What are you doing in here?"

"Hiding from the terror—whatever it is," gasped Rosie. "Oh, did you hear it? What is it? It sounds like a band of groaning giants. It woke me up. I sprang out of bed and thought of the closet. I just couldn't face it—whatever it is." She was chattering and trembling. Rosie was deadly afraid this time.

"There is nothing to face," said Carol, calmer and trying to be brave. "There is no one in this house but ourselves; we *know* that."

As if to disprove her words just then, there was

a slight sound and a movement at the far end of the hall.

"Oh!" cried Rosie, for she had left her room now and was out in the corridor with the other girls. "Oh, here it comes!"

"Stop it!" snapped Carol, whipping up a little anger. "It is only Rachel." And so it was. The housekeeper, more calm, it seemed, than any of them, was walking toward them, correctly attired, for that hour of the morning, in bathrobe and slippers and carrying the ever-present flashlight.

"Well," said Rachel, almost cheerfully, "it's here again."

"Yes," Carol said, "we certainly heard *It* this time. But I was just telling Rosie there is absolutely no one here, so what can harm us?"

"There *is* no one here. I saw to the locking-up myself," said the housekeeper. "But it might be well to make a search again. Those noises don't make themselves. Some one makes them." Even the valiant Rachel was now suspicious.

"That sounds sensible," said Carol. "But who on earth can it be?"

"Perhaps it is some one *not* of the earth," said Thally. She spoke more solemnly, perhaps, than she intended, for Rosie in a spasm of fear cried:

"Oh, I can't stand any more of it. I——"

The moans sounded again, but low and deep in tone, and far away—from below the very foundations of the old house, it seemed.

"They're going away," Carol said. "We had better investigate them before we lose all clews to the place where they come from."

"They're down cellar—I'm sure," Cecy declared.

"We'll go down once more," suggested Carol.

"I'm not going to stir a step unless we have a man with us!" announced Rosie. "And don't you girls dare go away and leave me. Get a man, can't you?" she wailed.

"We'll have Jensen in again, though I'm afraid he'll get angry at being disturbed so late," Carol said. "But I'll telephone."

While the others looked, waited and listened to the mysterious sounds now greatly lessened, Carol pushed the button which rang a bell on the telephone in Jensen's house. She had to push it several times before she heard the answering signal. Then the girls listened to the one-sided conversation.

"Yes, Jensen—this is Miss Duncan—yes—we are hearing the noises again—please come over—no, we aren't dreaming—do, please, come— Oh, yes—at once—you will? Thank you!" She hung up the receiver.

"He'll be right over," Carol said. "Rosie, get your robe on—we must all get our robes on," she added, for in the haste and excitement of the terror they were all in pajamas save the housekeeper.

"Oh, I'm not going down cellar with you!" Rosie declared, turning back to her room.

"Then you can stay up here—alone!" Carol warned her.

"Oh, no! Never! Don't you dare leave me!" cried Rosie.

"Then get your robe and we'll all go down together—with Jensen," ordered Carol, the leader.

In a few minutes there sounded a knock at the back door, and Jensen, with his lantern again, and a scornful grin on his somewhat sardonic face, came in.

"It all seems to be quiet now," he declared, after listening a moment as he stood in the kitchen surrounded by the girls and the housekeeper.

"It *is* quiet now," Carol agreed. "But you should have heard it. And it was different, this time."

"How different?" asked Jensen, picking up interest.

"Thumps and bumps," said Cecy. "As if someone was in the cellar and trying to get out and hammering everything in their way."

"Dogs," said Rachel, briefly.

"Then they must have been iron dogs," declared Thally.

"The noises and bumps certainly seemed to come from the cellar," stated Carol. "That's the logical place to look for causes."

"Come on, then," suggested Jensen, stepping toward the inner cellar door. "The outside one's locked, I suppose?" he asked.

"It was when we went to bed," stated Rachel. "Of course, I can't say but what some one may have opened it since then."

"I'll go outside and take a look," said the man. "Wait here."

"Oh, don't be afraid that we'll go down there alone!" said Rosie sarcastically.

"Afraid, eh?" asked the caretaker.

"Yes, and I don't care who knows it," Rosie answered. "It's all well enough to try to joke about this, but it's *no* joke."

"It may turn out so, after all," said Carol. "Of course, we all would have our opinions about the motives of a person who could perpetrate a joke like this," and she looked straight at Jensen.

"I'd like to get my hands on him—that's all I've got to say," the man declared. "Now I'll go take a look."

He hurried out with his lantern and came back in a short time to announce that the outside cellar door was securely fastened. Then they went down cellar, with Jensen in the lead but the result of their search was as before—there was no one in the cellar.

"Not so much as a rat!" Jensen said, and Rosie screamed a little as he said it. Clearly her nerves were, as Cecy said, "all shot."

Not so much as the whisper of a groan, a moan, a thump, or a bump was heard while they were in cellar. And when they went up, Jensen forming the rear guard, they stood for a moment in the kitchen.

"Well, what you want I should do now?" the caretaker asked peevishly.

"You can do nothing here," Carol said. "And if this is like any of the other times, the noises won't come back, so there's no need of keeping you any longer."

"No, I guess not," Jensen said. "But if you're going to be scared the rest of the night I can stay here—sleep on the sofa. My wife won't mind being left alone."

"Thank you, there is. no need for that," said Carol. "We can telephone you again if we need you to stay."

"Yes, I s'pose you can. Well—good-night."

He slithered out of the door with his bobbing light. Rachel locked it after him, bolted the inner cellar door and then faced the girls.

"Don't you want something to eat?" she asked as Rachel would.

"Eat!" exclaimed Thally, with a gesture of complete impossibility.

"Yes. It will probably make you sleep better. It will be quite a while until daylight and some hot milk and crackers——"

"A good idea, Rachel," decided Carol. "We certainly shall need some sleep. This thing sort of takes it out of you."

"If we can sleep after what happened," sighed

Rosie. "Oh, I don't want to seem fussy," she said, plaintively, "but really——"

"I know how you feel," interrupted Carol. "Don't worry, darling. We all feel the same. But Cecy and I, at least, must get to the bottom of this. Aunt Isabel——"

"Oh, I'll stay with you!" Rosie hastened to say.

"And I!" added Thally.

They did manage to fall asleep after the little lunch Rachel prepared, and in the morning they were almost inclined to doubt that anything had happened. But serious thought came back and made a reality of what had seemed only a shadow —or, more properly, perhaps, an echo.

"There's one thing we must do!" decided Carol after breakfast.

"What?" demanded Thally.

"We must do what the boys in camp would call 'stand guard,'" was the answer.

"You mean to get Glenn and Ted back here?" asked Cecy.

"Yes, if they'll come, and I think they will," said Carol. "If we can get them here, perhaps with one or two more, they can form a guard about the house, stay awake in relays and we will do the same inside the house and then, if the noises occur, as they may, we can eliminate the suspicion that some one outside is doing this to frighten us away."

"A good idea!" said Thally.

The more they talked it over and thought about

it the better and more logical it seemed. No time was lost in starting for Camp Tagawah and there Glenn and Ted fell in readily with the plan. They had made arrangements for staying away from camp for the night, so that night a guard was posted about the old house, while the girls took turns in sitting up to watch from within.

It was during the morning watch, when Glenn and Ted were patrolling, and when Carol and Thally were on guard inside, sitting in Carol's room, that the noises sounded again. This time there were just deep moans with, now and then, a high-pitched cry. Lights were quickly flashed on and when Glenn and Ted joined the girls they said not a person had approached the house from outside.

"Yet the noises are here," said Carol, now deeply concerned.

"Then they are made by someone inside the house," insisted Ted. "We heard them outside, but no one came near the place, we're sure of that."

"And there is no one inside the house who could do it," stated Carol. "Oh, it seems to be getting deeper—this awful mystery," she sighed, now completely discouraged herself.

"Well, it sure gets me!" said Glenn later, at a sort of final conference. "You'd better give this up, Carol. And it might be safer—to quit!"

"Never! I'm going to find out what it's all about. At least *It* doesn't harm us."

"Good girl! I wish you luck. And we'll come over again. It's just possible that someone slipped by us in the dark," Glenn tried to cheer them.

"Never!" declared Ted. "We didn't fall asleep once. My eyes sting."

"I'm sure you didn't," said Cecy. "But how could anyone, even in playing a trick, make such awful sounds?" she wanted to know.

"If that's a human voice, however magnified, then I'm a Chinaman!" declared Ted. "It was more like the bellow of a giant bull."

"Oh, that white cow—the one who we think scared Toledo, the colored boy!" cried Cecy. "Why not?"

"If a cow came around and used a glorified speaking tube, I'm another Chinaman!" said Glenn. "Girls, it's got us guessing." And indeed that at least was true.

But when three days passed, without a recurrence of the mysterious sounds, hope returned. Perhaps it was all ended. Even Rosie calmed enough to go up in the attic alone (though in broad daylight) to look for a small flax spinning wheel she said she wanted to buy from Aunt Isabel, if she would sell the relic.

"I believe she will," Carol said. "Aunt Isabel doesn't care much for such things. In fact, I think she might make quite a sum of money by getting rid of the old colonial relics up there, if she would bother to do it."

But Rosie did not bring down the spinning wheel. She had not been up in the dim attic more than a few minutes before the girls heard her scream in fear. Then she came dashing down the stairs crying:

"Oh! Oh! It almost got me!" Her face was pale. She was trembling.

"What was it?" asked Carol in surprise.

"The ghost! The ghost! The fluttering ghost!"

And then Rosie collapsed in a chair, her trembling hands held over her face to shut out even the memory of what she had seen.

CHAPTER XVI

DESERTION

CAROL DUNCAN decided that now, if ever, was a time to be firm. She took Rosie by the shoulders in a tense grip and spoke sharply.

"Now stop this! Tell us exactly what happened. You didn't see anything! Nothing nearly got you. You're just nervous and excited. Stop this silly nonsense and tell us!"

Something in Carol's voice, something in her grip, put calming pressure on Rosie's nerves so that she removed her hands from her face. She looked around at the circle of girls and said:

"But I did see something—not clearly, but it was *something*. It fluttered at me—swooped down from high up in the attic—among the rafters and came down. I could feel a strong wind blowing on me. It passed over my head. It stirred my hair. Then I screamed and came down! Oh. It was real! It was real!"

"Nonsense!" said Carol, though not with conviction.

"We had better go up to the attic and take a look," proposed Thally. "I'll go with you, Carol.

I'm not afraid." *This* was more like the old Thally.

"No, why should we be? Probably something that was hanging on the rafters—an old dress or something—fell off near Rosie. That would make a fluttering of the air," reasoned Carol, looking questioningly at the still frightened girl.

"It was no falling dress," Rosie declared. "I tell you it fluttered at me—swooped—with great force. It was like a strong wind blowing. Look at my hair!" Certainly it was all on end.

"Then I'm going up to look!" Carol decided.

"You stay with me, Cecy!" Rosie pleaded. "Don't you go!"

"Yes, dear, I'll stay with you. Oh, I do hope you find it," she said to Carol and Thally, as they started toward the attic stairs. Here was a new and different menace.

"You do? Hope you find it!" cried Rosie, incredulously.

"Yes. It might explain all that's been happening here," Cecy tried to explain.

Carol and Thally did not pause to comment on this. They went straight up into the attic. Soon Cecy and Rosie could hear them tramping around. They did not stay long, however, and when they descended, their faces showed no triumph of discovery. Thally shook her head slowly and Carol said:

"We could find nothing."

"Not some garment or big piece of fluttery cloth that had fallen from a rafter?" asked Cecy.

"Not a thing."

"I told you it was a *ghost*," exclaimed Rosie triumphantly.

"Well, I guess we'll have to let it go that way—for the present," Carol said. "It certainly is—mystifying."

It was next morning that Carol, passing Rosie's room, saw her busily packing.

"What are you doing?" Carol asked in surprise.

"Getting my things together," said Rosie, meekly.

"What for?"

"I'm going to leave."

"Leave! Oh. Rosie!"

"Yes, Carol, dear! Oh, I can't stand it! My nerves are all on a ragged edge. I don't want to seem mean, and you know how fond I am of you all and how I'd love to stay here if—if things were different."

"Yes, I know. I had no idea it would be such a strenuous matter when I asked you to come up here with us," Carol assured her.

"Neither did I. It seemed as though it would be lovely. And I'm so fond of the sea—I just love bathing. But with those quicksands down there, and the noises and that ghost in the attic— Oh, Carol, I can't stand it! I'm going home!"

Carol was stunned for the moment, but she

rallied herself bravely, as she always did and met the situation calmly.

"Perhaps if you stay just another day or two this may all be explained, Rosie," she said, encouragingly.

"No! No! I'm sorry, but I can't wait. I must go home! I'll be a wreck if I stay any longer."

Carol could not deny this. "All right, my dear," she said quietly. "I'll help you pack and Cecy can go with you."

"Oh, I don't need anyone—really."

"Yes, Cecy must go. I'll call her—we'll both help you pack."

"I really don't need Cecy," Rosie declared, "but I feel I must go. Oh, it's awful to desert you this way, Carol, but——"

"Not at all. I can understand how you feel. You really are worried, and I wouldn't think of letting you drive back to Melody Lane alone. Cecy must go with you. She can come back if she wants to."

But, most unexpectedly, Cecy said she would be glad to go with Rosie only she wasn't coming back!

"Not coming back?" gasped Thally when she heard the news.

"No!" Cecy was almost as firm as the departing guest. "I'm fed up with this, if you don't mind me saying so, Carol. Let Aunt Isabel come back here and clear out her own ghosts and noises! I've had enough."

This was indeed a surprise but Carol was firm. "Very well," she said, quietly, "perhaps it will be best that way. Get ready, Cecy. It's a long drive and you must start at once."

"You are sure you won't mind, Carol?" asked the younger sister, plaintively.

"Well, of course I'll miss you two—so will Thally." Carol glanced at her chum who confirmed this by a little nod. "But Thally and I will carry on," Carol answered for both.

"Oh, are you surely going to stay—you two— alone in this awful house?" asked Rosie, snapping her suitcase shut, noisily.

"We shan't be alone—Rachel will be with us— Jensen is within call and the boys will come over whenever we need them," asserted Carol.

"I think you're silly to stay here," decided Cecy, "but I'm glad you aren't making a fuss about our going. Come on, Rosie; we'll be home by night and get some sleep without lying awake listening for ghost noises. And am I deaf and dumb from scares!"

"Yes, that's it," Rosie sighed. "It's the awful terror of the night that I can't stand."

So Rosie deserted, and Cecy went with her.

CHAPTER XVII

THE ATTIC SECRET

WHEN Glenn and Ted, again obtaining a few hours off, came over to see the girls at Rocky Cliff that afternoon, they were surprised to find only Carol and Thally with Rachel, at the old house.

"Where's Rosie—and Cecy?" demanded Glenn. "And what's worrying you?" he asked Carol, while Ted devoted himself, for the moment, to the radiant Thally.

"How do you know anything is worrying me?" countered Carol.

"I can tell by your face. Come on, out with it!"

"That's it—two are out."

"You're still one to the good—I should say two," and Glenn looked over where Thally and Ted were talking pleasantly. "But do you mean that Cecy——"

"She's gone—with Rosie. Rosie decided she had to leave. Couldn't stand it."

"So—she couldn't take it!" said Glenn and, though he laughed a little, there was a serious look on his face.

172

"It seems she couldn't—after what happened in the attic."

"What happened?"

Carol then told of the attic adventure.

"Well, I think she might have stuck it out just the same," Glenn said. "But of course, Rosie——"

"Rosie is Rosie," interrupted Carol.

"But what about Cecy?" asked Glenn.

"Well, I believe Cecy would have stayed on but for Rosie," admitted Carol. "And it made it look a little better for poor Rosie to have Cecy admit that things were getting on her nerves, too. It sort of—well—you know what I mean. She seemed pretty well scared herself," Carol admitted.

"Are you satisfied to have them both gone?"

"Yes. I guess so. But that doesn't explain it."

"Explain what?"

"The attic secret—ghost—or whatever it is."

"That's right," admitted Glenn. "Well, suppose Ted and I have a shot at that."

"I don't believe you can discover anything. We couldn't, and we went up and looked around thoroughly," said Carol.

"Well, we'll try," offered Glenn. "Come on, Ted," he called to his chum.

"Where now?" Ted was, obviously, having a good time with Thally and reluctant to leave.

"Up in the attic. We've got to dig out a ghost."

"I'm with you! Bring on your ghost!" challenged Ted.

The two young men were soon climbing the attic stairs, while Thally and Carol waited below. They could hear the two talking, laughing and warning each other to be careful, to keep fingers crossed and such nonsense.

"I don't see what they can possibly find up there," Carol remarked to Thally. "But I don't see what can be up there to have frightened Rosie so."

"She certainly was frightened," Thally agreed.

Suddenly they heard Glenn shout: "I've got him! I've—got—him!"

"Look out he doesn't claw you!" yelled Ted.

"There he goes!" sang out Glenn.

There was the tinkling sound of breaking glass, a rush of feet, thuds and shouts and then Glenn called:

"Well, he's out, anyhow!"

"He must have broken his neck diving through the window that way!" exclaimed Ted.

"Oh, what do you think it was?" Thally whispered to Carol.

"I haven't the least idea. But we'll soon know."

Glenn and Ted rushed downstairs.

"Well, we found it," Glenn announced merrily.

"The ghost?" Carol gasped.

"Ghost!" Glenn laughed. "Ghost nothing! It was a great, big, white owl!"

"Owl!"

"Yes. One of the largest I've ever seen. No wonder it scared poor Rosie nearly out of her wits when it swooped, swoshed or fluttered at her—whatever best describes an owl's antics."

"But an owl—in the attic?" questioned Thally.

"No better place for an owl," affirmed Ted. "Attics are the best places known to science for owls. This one must have gotten in and couldn't get out again. Probably flew in when a window was open and couldn't get out when it was closed."

"Yes, Rachel did open some windows to air the place," Carol recalled. "And I suppose the bird could have come in that way. And I remember Rachel going up to close the windows rather late one evening."

"Just about the time the owl was going out for his evening fly," said Glenn. "That must be how it happened. But the critter got so flustered when he saw two bright young men, he flew right at us. And he was big enough to put up a good fight, too."

"His beak was a hook and his claws razor sharp, I'm sure," said Ted. "He seemed to shoot down out of some dark corner."

"Where he stayed during the day," added Glenn, "probably trying to figure a way out. I made a grab for him when he swooped, but it is probably just as well I didn't get hold of him. Then he made a shot for the window."

"And got a bullseye!" laughed Ted. "You'll have to get the glass man in, Carol."

"I'll be glad to if that solves the secret of the attic."

"It does—don't worry," said Glenn.

"Do you suppose it was the owl of the attic who made all the terrifying noises?" asked Thally, hopefully.

Glenn did not answer for a moment. When he did he said:

"No, I don't believe it was. The real mystery still remains to be solved."

CHAPTER XVIII

DOWN THE CHUTE

WITH the attic angle cleared up, the party concentrated upon the real mystery.

Talk it over as the girls did with the boys during the remainder of the afternoon call, they arrived at no solution. Carol told Glenn and Ted all she had heard from Aunt Isabel, all that Jensen had related and all she herself and Thally had heard. She mentioned the terrorizing noises of the first night, which she and Rachel had kept secret for a time.

It was during the remainder of the boys' afternoon visit that Carol explained her first fright; that which Rachel shared.

"At first I think I was inclined to believe that Rachel may have had a nightmare," Carol said. "But later we talked it over and, in view of what has happened since, we now know it must have been the Terror—that first night."

"Terror! What Terror?" scoffed Ted.

"It does seem like something to laugh at," stated Glenn. "But you can't laugh away the sounds we ourselves heard. I'll leave Toledo the dark boy, out of it—I think some animal scared him—just what, makes little difference. But since he said it laughed at him it might have been a horse. They whinnie, you know."

"You haven't seen the little fellow since, have you?" asked Ted.

"Not right around here," Carol answered. "Though I did notice him in the village once or twice. He was not up to any tricks and has nothing to do with our real troubles, I'm sure of that. He's just a silly little boy."

"He might have been put up to it by someone," Ted suggested. He seemed to want to simplify matters.

"Who would put him up to it?" asked Thally, in surprise.

"Well, I seem to remember Carol saying something about her aunt being obliged to either live in this place herself, or make some profitable use of it. If she didn't, it goes to some other branch of the family, doesn't it?"

"Yes," Carol admitted, "to a Mr. Sim Rollinson, who lives over in Glendola, I believe. Mr. Rollinson is a half brother to Aunt Isabel. They don't get along very well, I believe."

"Glendola is about five miles from camp," stated Glenn. "I took some of the boys on a hike there the other day. So Mr. Rollinson stands a chance to get Rocky Cliff, is that it, Carol?"

"Yes, under certain conditions—one being that Aunt Isabel can't use the place beyond a certain time—I believe the time is up this fall. I didn't pay much attention to that part of it. Aunt Isabel mentioned it, but I never really thought we should find any serious conditions here so I took no family history notes."

As it came time for the boys to leave Carol asked if they might be safe from the ghostly white owl.

"He isn't likely to come back after the scare I gave him," Glenn assured her. "Still it wouldn't be a bad idea to stuff up that broken window, just in case, you know. We'll stuff it up for you," he offered.

"Oh, by all means, yes!" exclaimed Thally. "It will be bad enough to wake up in the night and hear the down cellar groans without hearing the attic whirrs. At least we know that the cellar sounds can't get up and grab us."

"As the Chinese warrior might do!" half laughed Carol. "And when you finish stuffing up that broken window for us, boys, will you wheel his Royal Highness, or whatever his title is, into the big hall closet? We are taking no more chances."

The window was made tight against another invasion of the great, white owl and then the boys prepared to shift the warrior. He stood upon a pedestal which rolled on castors, so it was easy enough to move.

"He sure is no beauty," remarked Glenn, as he scrutinized the evil, grinning mask of a face with the dangling horsehair about it.

"How would you like to wake up and find him bending over you?" asked Thally. Her fears brought fascination.

"Not so good!" admitted Ted. "Come on, Glenn, let's give him a ride."

They started to oust the armored figure when, suddenly, Carol stopped them with an exclamation.

"What is it?" Glenn asked.

"I know it's rather silly," she replied, "but would you boys, while you are at it, look inside that suit of mail and see if it is empty."

"Why, what do you mean?" asked Ted in surprise. "The warrior who wore it must be dust and ashes long ago. Even the most orthodox Chinese don't use this sort of armor any more. They have airplanes and machine guns over there," he explained.

"Please pull it apart, just the same," begged Carol. "We may sleep better for knowing for certain there is no one hidden in there to make ghostly noises. Not even a mummy."

The boys laughed but went at the task. They lifted up the pieces of hinged metal that formed protection for the warrior's thighs, they pulled aside the mask and looked back of it and Ted even ran the blade of his knife in the joints of the arm protectors. But the armor was untenanted. It was merely hung upon a wooden framework, in order to be exhibited in the manner in which it was worn.

"Not even a skeleton in it. Just a show-off," laughed Glenn. "Are you satisfied now, Carol?"

"Oh, yes. Put it away," she sighed. The old thing made her nervous.

So the Chinese armor, really a valuable museum piece, was wheeled into the depths of a big, empty closet at the far end of the hall. Then Carol locked the door and took out the key.

"You surely are taking no chances!" laughed Ted.

"No," she answered, "I am not."

Then the boys had to hurry off.

Supper, with only Carol and Thally at the table, was rather a lonesome meal in Rocky Cliff that evening, though the two girls made the best of it. Even Rachel, perhaps sensing their mood, offered a sample of her jokes and the girls were glad enough to laugh over them. And they were glad also when the telephone suddenly rang. Both of them hurried to answer it.

"It's Cecy!" announced Carol, successful in the race to reach the receiver.

"Is anything the matter?" asked Thally, anxiously.

"No," said Carol, after listening, "she just wanted to let us know that she and Rosie are safely back in Melody Lane."

"Oh," murmured Thally. And she listened

while Carol told what news there was of happenings since the girls' departure that morning. And that was that.

It seemed to Carol and Thally that Rachel was unusually careful about locking up that night. But perhaps they were over sensitive. But all night nothing happened. Not a sound was heard, and although she felt it could not be so, Carol was almost ready to declare that the departure of the owl and the closeting of the Chinese warrior might have ended the weird noises. If only it would prove to be true!

When two more days had passed, and nothing happened, the girls were almost ready to believe that the "thing" as they called it, had decided to leave them in peace.

"I was getting ready to suggest that we get that young engineer and his sister to come and stay with us, now that Cecy and Rosie are away—what's his name?" asked Thally.

"Oh, you mean Barry Brennan," said Carol.

"Yes. Have you seen him since the accident—or his sister?"

"I saw them in the village once or twice. The injured leg is better, so Mr. Brennan can hobble about. He and his sister promised to call."

"I hope they do. I rather liked him—them, I mean," said Thally.

"They were nice, yes. And, speaking of him, let's do what we planned to do some time ago."

"What's that?" asked Carol.

"Have a better look around the old mill. Really we didn't go in, you know."

"All right, let's go. Only not around that dangerous wheel," protested Thally.

"No, we'll leave that alone after what happened to Mr. Brennan. It might be jinxed."

It was toward the middle of the afternoon when Carol and Thally, telling Rachel where they were bound for, headed toward the old mill. Though considerable of a ruin, there were some parts of it that could easily be entered from low doors along what once must have been a lane up which carts of grain were driven. Now the lane was overgrown with grass and weeds.

"It still seems to have the musty smell of old flour," said Carol, as she and Thally entered.

"Doesn't it. How quaint!" and Thally began to examine some of the many bins that had once held grain, meal, flour or whatever was the grist that was ground. The girls peered down dim, dusty shafts and had glimpses of ancient machinery now almost all rotted or rusted away. But the wooden parts of such a mill are made of timber to withstand the ravages of time.

"What do you suppose this hole in the floor was for?" asked Thally as she stepped gingerly toward a square, black shaft.

"I don't know—let's take a look," Carol offered, stepping toward her chum. There was no cover to the hole, or shaft, and both girls were careful not to go too near, for the old boards of the mill were slippery from years of tramping feet and from the hauling of bags of dusty meal across them, they were fairly glazed from the oils of grain.

"It seems to have been a sort of grain chute," Carol decided. "I think the farmers brought their grain in on this floor and it was dropped down this chute to the grinding millwheels below. Ugh! It looks ugly, doesn't it?"

"Black and ghostly," agreed Thally. "Let's get out of here."

She turned and Carol turned to follow her, but at that moment something like a great shadowy arm seemed to pass between the girls. It struck Carol in the back and, in an instant she was precipitated down the old grain chute! Her terrified screams rang in Thally's ears and echoed throughout the dim, old mill.

Carol was down in the chute!

CHAPTER XIX

A GREAT CRASH

THALLY's cry of terror and alarm followed close on Carol's shout of dismay, as she felt herself slipping down into the depths of that terrifying blackness.

"Carol! Carol!" Thally screamed. "Oh! Mercy!"

There was no answer.

Involuntarily Thally looked up and then all around her. There was no sign of any intruder— no evidence that anyone had entered to push Carol down that chute. Yet Thally was sure she had seen something like a great arm swooping through the air.

"Carol! Carol! Are you hurt? Is there any way you can get up?" yelled Thally.

For a few seconds in which Thally's heart beat madly, there was no answer. She began to fear the worst and she was on the point of deciding to run out and summon help. But she called once more:

"Carol! Carol!"

To her relief the voice answered and vigorously

enough to give evidence that at least Carol was not seriously hurt. Indeed she said:

"I'm all right. I'm not hurt a bit but I'm a regular dust rag."

"Oh, how glad I am!" breathed Thally. "But where are you?"

"I seem to be jammed and shut up in some sort of a box," Carol's voice came echoingly up out of the chute. "I think I must have slid feet first into a grain bin but I can't seem to find my way out. I'm on a floor below you. If you can go outside you might find a door to this place. Then maybe you can open the bin." Carol's words were broken by her excitement.

"I'll try—right away!" breathlessly promised Thally. "You won't mind if I leave up here?"

"Not at all. You can't do any good up there without a rope. I think you can easily open the bin from outside and then I can wiggle out. Only do hurry. I'm nearly smothered with the dust I kicked up."

"Coming, Carol, dear! Coming!"

Thally ran out of the mill, gave a hasty look around hoping she might see Jensen or someone to whom she could appeal for help, but seeing no one, she ran down a little hill toward the back of the mill.

Carol's guess was right. There was a lower door to the old structure. It had fallen from its hinges thus affording easy access for Thally and the setting sun reflected bright and reassuring rays within. Before her Thally saw a number of great wooden boxes, all shut with doors that could be raised and lowered in grooves. She did not know which of these boxes, or bins, that had once held the ground grist, now imprisoned Carol.

Thally, to settle the matter called loudly:

"Carol! Carol! Kick against the sides!"

Carol understood and obeyed. Thus the centre of five great bins was identified. Thally sprang to it and, using the lever that was evidently there for the purpose, succeeded, after some effort, in raising the sliding door. Then Carol, a strange, dusty and disheveled figure half crept, half rolled out.

"Oh, thank goodness!" she murmured as she stood upright and shook herself like a dog emerging from the water. A little aura of dust surrounded her.

"Carol, dear, are you sure you're not hurt?" demanded Thally.

"Not in the least. Not even bruised. It was like going down the chute at some picnic ground."

Then, as they went back up into the mill and made a more calm examination of the apparatus, the terrifying details of what had happened were made plain.

Over Thally's head, and back of Carol as she stood on the brink of the chute, peering into its depths, was a big wooden lever, once used in the mill work—probably for opening a damper in some overhead grain chute or in starting or stopping the machinery like a belt-shifter in a factory.

It was this great wooden lever, truly like a giant's arm, that, in some unexpected manner moving in a wide arc, had struck Carol between her shoulders and literally thrust her down the shaft.

"Oh, I'm so glad it was that—something tangible instead of a ghost!" gasped Thally as she leaned over the square, black opening, taking care not to get in the way of the lever and not to approach too close to the edge of that chute which was, for all she knew, a bottomless pit. "Carol, you must have stepped on some spring that worked that lever." She looked for something of this nature on the floor, but saw nothing.

"No more of this mill for me!" decided Carol when she had, with the help of her chum, gotten rid of the dust, had straightened out her clothes and both were out in the open.

"I should say not!" agreed Thally. "First Mr. Brennan gets hurt here and then you mysteriously vanish from my sight. What did you think when you began to fall?"

"I didn't have time to do much thinking, my child. But I did have a flash of fear when I thought someone, with evil intentions, had pushed me. I don't yet know for sure what it was."

"It was that great, wooden arm, I'm sure," said Thally. "I didn't exactly *see* it but I'm sure that's what it was."

"Perhaps," Carol admitted. "I felt some sort of a thump. But we can't call this part of the mystery. It's just a natural happening."

"That's all to be said for it," Thally remarked. "But it was a major scare, all right, and proves that mere females should keep out of the way of vast machines, even old grist mills."

That night at the Cliff, like several preceding, passed in blessed quiet. Really the girls needed some respite from the terrorizing alarms, grimly determined though they were to get at the bottom of the mystery.

The following day was passed pleasantly in going to the boys' camp, on invitation from Glenn and Ted, and witnessing some late summer water and land sports. It made a welcome break in their vacation which, up to now, could hardly have been called merry.

But this particular day that had been gay and happy, filled with sunshine, was not followed by so lovely a night. A severe thunderstorm broke soon after supper and then came a flood of rain.

"I hope the roof doesn't leak," murmured Thally, as she and Carol crept up to bed. Rachel had gone up first, after her usual care in locking up and closing windows against the storm.

"Even if the roof leaked, it would only be the attic that could get wet," said Carol.

"The owless attic," murmured Thally gratefully.

They read a while in bed, called back and forth

from their rooms, and then, with the usual hall light bulb left aglow, and with flashlights under their pillows, also as usual, the two girls managed to sleep.

But not for long, for about midnight the Terror sounded again. The awful moans—not shrill shrieks this time—just low moans as if someone was suffering untold agony!

"Oh! OH!" screamed Thally, fairly leaping from bed. "Oh——"

"I'm here—don't be afraid!" called Rachel's voice.

Carol opened her door. "They're back!" she said, grimly, her electric light making herself look ghostly in her silvery robe.

Then, as they listened to the moans dying away suddenly the whole house vibrated as a great crash sounded—a crash of rending wood and a rattle as of a table of dishes upset on the floor.

Rachel rushed to them.

"There, dears!" she murmured trying to protect both girls with her willing arms, "don't get excited."

CHAPTER XX

MISSING

MOMENTARILY paralyzed with fright, actually bereft of the power to move for the first few seconds following that tremendous sound, Carol, Thally and Rachel stood in the upper hall. Even the grim, iron nerves of the Scotchwoman were shattered, Carol could see that, for Rachel too was shaky.

An intense silence followed the crash and the moans that had preceded it, a silence so deep that they could all hear the ticking of the big grandfather's clock down in the living room.

Then Thally spoke in a tense, hoarse voice:

"What was it? Oh, Carol, what was it?"

"I don't know."

"But we'll find out!" declared Rachel stoutly. "Come on!"

She moved toward the head of the stairs.

"It sounded like—like the end of the world," whispered Thally again clutching at Carol.

They knew that it was still raining hard and that the wind was blowing a gale. The sea would be kicking up a fuss now. But the lightning had ceased flashing and the thunder had stopped rumbling.

"Wait!" exclaimed Carol when Rachel was at the head of the stairs.

"Why?" inquired the housekeeper. "Don't you want to find out what that noise was?"

"Yes," Carol answered, "but we must put on our slippers and you your robe, Rachel." For once the meticulous housekeeper, Rachel, had appeared upon the scene just as she had leaped out of bed when the crash came, in a stout muslin gown.

"Oh, yes, of course." Rachel started back toward her room.

"Maybe it was an earthquake," Thally said.

"We never have them in this part of the country," Carol reminded her.

"Then the house was struck by lightning."

"I hope it turns out to be as simple as that, Thally. But if lightning had struck the house, or near it, we'd have felt a much worse shock than we did, I imagine."

"True enough," said Rachel coming from her room now more thickly clad. "And you'd smell sulphur and feel something like pins and needles all over you. A place where I lived was struck once and that's just how it was."

"Anyhow," went on Thally as she and Carol, now robed and slippered went toward the stairs, "I think we ought to get Jensen over here. We need a man this time if ever."

"I'll see if I can get him on the telephone," Carol offered.

But to all her ringings there was no answer. The instrument was dead.

"Wires probably down in the storm," said Carol. "Come on. We know, from past experience that we never see anyone—or anything—after those moans," she insisted.

"But the crash was different," argued Thally.

"Well, let's find out. Forward, march!" Carol smiled as she gave this command, like whistling to keep courage up.

With flashlights glowing, all three of them did march like a parade. Carol switched on the lower lights from the upper hall, and they tramped down the big stairway. Cautiously they looked around but could not see what had caused the terrible crash.

Then, as Carol looked into the dining room the cause of the big noise was discovered. An old cherry corner cupboard, really an antique piece, had fallen forward from where it had stood many years against the wall, and had crashed to the floor, smashing the glass doors and wrecking into sad conglomeration the pieces of glass and porcelain it had held.

"Look! Look!" cried Thally in a tense voice.

"Oh, that lovely closet!" murmured Rachel. "And all those nice dishes, and cups and saucers and glasses— Terrible!"

Pieces of the antique collection in that shattered cupboard were scattered far over the dining room floor.

"Be careful of broken glass!" warned Carol. "A sharp point could pierce our slippers. Careful!"

They walked gingerly about the room and Rachel said:

"I'll get a broom and sweep the worst of it up. In the morning I'll make a better job of it. But that lovely cupboard! It must be nearly a hundred years old and now it's broken. And there were some valuable dishes there too."

"They're not very valuable now," said Carol with a little smile. "However, I'm glad it's Aunt Isabel's property and not that of some stranger from whom we might have rented this place."

"Did your aunt set much of a store by this?" asked Rachel as she came in with broom and dustpan from the kitchen.

"I don't really believe she even knows it is here," said Carol. "She would hardly be keen on antiques —too much of a business woman, I guess. But what I'd like to know is, how this happened."

"It seemed securely fastened to the walls," said Thally. "And yet it looks as if someone—or something—had deliberately pulled or pushed it from its place."

"The vibration of some thunder clap might have done it," said Rachel. She always looked for a natural explanation of anything strange that occurred.

"There were some heavy blasts," Carol answered, "but I don't recall one severe enough to have knocked over this cupboard. Besides, this fell only a little while ago, and the storm was over then—except for the wind and rain." The reasoning was sound; but what had caused the crash?

"More mystery," sighed Thally. "We've got to do something about it now. This is the limit!"

"It does seem so," agreed Carol. "Well, we'll have Jensen in as soon as it's daylight and see if he can explain it. He has been about this old house for years."

"Do you mean the cupboard may have a habit of falling over?" suggested Thally, laughing a little nervously.

"Well, no—not that exactly. But we'll ask Jensen. Maybe *he* knows."

"And get Glenn and Ted over again, too," Thally begged. "This may be something they can figure out even if they can't discover the source of the moans."

"We'll do that," Carol agreed. "But there's no use going down cellar now. We wouldn't find anything—see anything——"

"You wouldn't get me down cellar tonight, not if you called out the National Guard!" declared Thally. "We might not *see* anything but we'd be pretty certain to *hear* something, and my nerves won't stand anything more."

"No, we shouldn't try them to the limit," agreed Carol. "Things seem going from bad to worse," she added, looking at the fallen cupboard. "If we have many more scenes like this there won't be any house left for Aunt Isabel to worry about."

They stood for a moment, all three looking at the scene of small ruin about the cupboard. Rachel had swept up the scattered glass and china into a neat heap about the fallen mass of wood.

"There," the housekeeper said, "no use doing anything more until morning. Better get back to sleep."

"Sleep!" gasped Thally. "As if we could!"

"We must!" insisted Carol. "We have a task ahead of us. And we've got to go on with it."

"And I'm with you!" announced Thally loyally. "Perhaps I shall sleep, after all."

"We can only try," concluded Carol, rather pathetically.

They left the disordered dining room and went up stairs. The rain was easing up now, and the wind going down. The night grew quieter. No more moans came from beneath the great house.

When morning came—a bright, beautiful morning, Rachel was up early, and Carol, hearing her moving about in the dining room concluded she ought to go down and supervise the permanent removal of the broken glass and porcelain. She found Rachel standing over the fallen cupboard which was lying on the place where the leaded glass doors had been. Now the lead was twisted and the glass shattered. The housekeeper had gathered into a basket a pile of broken fragments.

"We can't do anything with them," she told Carol.

"We'll put the pieces in the big closet where we hid the Chinese warrior," Carol decided. "I'll write to Aunt Isabel about what happened. Wait, I'll unlock the door, Rachel, and you can store the pieces in the closet, together with the others we pick out when Jensen comes in to put the cupboard back in place. Something might be done with the pieces."

Carol opened the closet door. Rachel stood behind her with the basket of débris. And then, as the portal swung open Carol had another shock.

The ugly, evil, masked face of the ancient celestial fighter was gone. The whole suit of armor was missing. Yet the closet door had been locked and Carol had the key in her room!

CHAPTER XXI

THE LADIES PROTEST

THALLY, who had just come down stairs, noticed Rachel and Carol standing in front of the strangely empty closet. There was something in the attitudes of the two—something of fear undefined, that set Thally's heart madly to pounding, as it had in the night.

"Is—has anything—what's the matter?" she finally burst out.

"Yes, something has happened," said Carol in a low voice. "Something very strange. The warrior is gone!"

"Gone!" Thally almost screamed the word.

"Yes. Look!" Carol and Rachel stepped back so Thally might have an unobstructed view of the place where the evil armored figure had stood upon the castored pedestal. Now even the pedestal was gone.

"Where did it go—who took it?" Thally demanded almost indignantly, though there was a feeling of relief in her heart that the "Chinese demon," as she often called him, was no longer there.

"We don't know," Carol said in a dull, toneless

voice. "Rachel and I came here to put away the pieces from the closet; we thought possibly some of them might be cemented together again. The closet was locked as it has been since we put the thing away." Carol felt justified in calling the armored warrior a "thing." She went on: "I got the key and opened it. We found the place empty. And I know no one has had a chance to get the key, for I hid it and it was in a place no one would, ordinarily think to look. It was there, just as I had left it. But the *thing* is gone!"

"The last straw!" murmured Thally, ready to sink down in discouragement.

"What do you mean—last straw?" asked Carol quickly.

"I'll tell you later. Just now we must get Jensen in and see if he can explain the disappearance of Ching Sow, or whatever his name was, and also about the falling cupboard. You get Jensen, Carol. I'll go with you in a moment. I suppose his telephone is still out of order."

While Thally and the housekeeper stood eying with fears and misgivings, the place where the Chinese warrior had been hidden, Carol attempted to telephone.

"There may be an explanation to this," Thally said, rather vaguely.

"What?" asked Rachel.

"The disappearance of the warrior. Jensen knew how we hated the sight of it and he may have come and taken it away in the night. He may even have knocked the cupboard over by accident." Thally's voice told how much she hoped this explanation would prove correct.

But Rachel shook her head. "There was no human being in this house last night but us," she declared. "I saw to the locking up. All the doors and windows were tightly fastened when I came down this morning. Besides, Carol had the closet key. And another thing, Jensen never could have taken that image away by himself. It was too heavy."

"That's so," said Thally, remembering how Glenn and Ted had struggled to put it in the closet even on the rolling castors.

They lapsed into silence as they heard Carol trying to phone, but the local line was still out of order.

"How about Jensen? We will have to go out for him," Thally suggested.

They found the caretaker on his way to the house. He had tried to telephone early in the morning, to ask if the storm had done any damage to Rocky Cliff. Finding the telephone "dead," he set out to trace the wire and had just found the break when the girls met him.

"The storm did no damage, as far as we have seen," Carol told him, "but something terrible happened, Jensen."

"You mean the moans again?" He grinned sardonically.

"Yes, the moans, and then some ghost got in and tore down the corner cupboard and smashed a lot of dishes!" burst out Thally.

"A ghost got in?" cried the caretaker. This time he did not laugh.

"Well, it was something. Come and see."

"All right—I will. But I wouldn't let that cupboard worry me. It's been on the point of toppling over for a year. I've always been minded to nail it back in place but I forgot it—not thinking it would be needed again."

"Do you think that explains it?" asked Carol.

"I'm sure it will, miss. That cupboard was very teetery on its base, and some of the old nails that fastened it to the corner walls were rusted away. A good clap of thunder would send it toppling— very likely did. I can tell when I look at it."

"Well, that'll be that! Thanks for a little relief from the general horror," murmured Thally. "But what about the Chinese figure?"

"Eh?" asked the caretaker sharply, looking from one girl to the other.

"The suit of Chinese armor disappeared out of the closet where it was locked," said Carol. "Did you, by any chance, take it away, Jensen?"

"Who, me? No, indeed. I'd never touch the thing. If 'twas mine I'd have heaved it into the

bay, off the cliff, long ago. Or even into the quicksands—that's the proper place for it—the quicksands. But it isn't my property—belongs to the
doctor, though where he is I don't know. I believe
the sight of that devilish face helped to send that
one patient to his death. No, I wouldn't touch the
Chinese."

"Then where did it go?" asked Thally.

"I can't tell you, but it'll do no harm for me to
take a look at the closet." He was now genuinely
interested.

"Please do," urged Carol, and they started for
the house.

Jensen's visit to the mansion proved one thing.
He was right about the cupboard. The holding
nails had rusted away—the cupboard was, indeed,
insecure on its base, and even the girls could understand how a clap of thunder, like some of those
which had shaken the house, could vibrate the dish
closet down. They were satisfied at least on this
point.

"But how did the Chinese warrior escape?" asked
Thally.

That was not so easily answered. Indeed, it
could not be answered at all, just then. With Jensen the girls examined the closet, using their flashlights. The floor showed no marks other than
those of the castors when the pedestal was rolled
in. There was no evidence that the door had been

unlocked and locked again; no evidence that the bulky, heavy figure had been spirited away in the night. Yet it was gone.

"Well, I can't help you about this," Jensen said grimly. "It's a puzzle to me. But I should think you'd be glad to have the evil thing out of the house," he attempted to reason.

"We are," said Thally. "But if some one can sneak in during the night and make away with the armor, they might do something worse."

"That wouldn't be easy, miss," grinned the caretaker. "Not but what either or both of you are worth stealing!" and he laughed rather pleased at his joke. "No, I can't explain. But I'll do anything you want. Just name it."

"That's just it," Thally said. "We don't know what we can do."

"We'll see you again, Jensen, before night," Carol said as she and her chum walked out of the dismal, big hall. "You will have your private telephone line repaired at once, won't you?"

"Oh, yes, miss. I'll be within call."

The two girls went out on the porch and Jensen went back to his work. For a little while both were silent, then Thally asked:

"Do you believe in anything like evil spirits, Carol?"

"Evil spirits—what do you mean?"

"Well, I can't help feeling that there was an evil

spirit in that suit of Chinese armor. Perhaps the ghost of the warrior who might have been killed while wearing it a thousand years ago."

"So what, my dear?" But Carol was smiling.

"Well, granting such a thing, suppose it was the evil spirit in the armor that has been doing the moaning, the shrieking and screaming? And suppose that now, its mission ended, it decided to go away and take its earthly home with it? Wouldn't that account for it?"

"If you grant the first of the fantastic themes you have to admit the rest," Carol said. "But I can't agree. Still there is something weird and queer about this place. I wonder if we shall ever understand it?"

"I'm not going to try!" said Thally, with decision.

"What—what are you going to do?" asked Carol, a feeling of something like panic within her.

"I don't know yet—I can't quite make up my mind. I said I wouldn't desert you and I won't— but we've got to have some protection here—at night. Now let's forget it all for a while and talk it over again this afternoon, when we can think more clearly."

"Not a bad idea," said Carol.

It was later that same afternoon, when Carol and Thally were sitting on the front porch, that they saw three prim little old ladies coming up the path. Obviously they were natives of Cedarshore.

One, who was more prim and severe looking than her companions bowed stiffly as they reached the bottom of the steps, and asked:

"Are you the young ladies who are living here?"

"Yes," Carol answered. "This is my Aunt Isabel's house. We are staying here for a time in her absence. Did you wish to see her?"

"No, thank you, we came to see you," said the prim one on the leader's left.

"To see us!" Carol tried to smile beamingly, and with welcome. But she was clearly puzzled. Cedarshore natives were not in the habit of calling at Rocky Cliff.

"We came," said the third member of the delegation, "to protest. We think you should go away from here. Our town is suffering from the ghostly reputation of this place and we feel you should leave."

CHAPTER XXII

BRAVE DECISION

CAROL and Thally were dumbfounded at such
a request. But quickly recovering her poise Carol
remembered her manners and said:

"Won't you please come up and sit down? I'm
sure you must be warm from your walk." And as
the ladies advanced to the porch where there were
sufficient rockers for all, Carol added: "This is
my friend Thalia Bond. I am Carol Duncan.
Miss Isabel Duncan is my father's aunt. I am
here at her request to——"

"Excuse me," spoke the taller and, seemingly,
the leading lady, "we know why you came, but it is
of no avail and may be dangerous." This was said
very deliberately.

"Besides keeping our whole little peaceful community on tenter hooks," added the shorter of the
trio. "Isn't that so, Abigail?" She appealed to
the remaining member of the delegation.

"Yes," was the gentle-voiced answer. "That
seems to state the case."

"But what is it all about?" asked Carol. "I'm

206

afraid I don't understand. We certainly don't want to disrupt Cedarshore. As for danger——"

"Believe me there is danger!" interrupted the tall lady. "We have heard what nearly happened to that poor little colored boy."

"Nothing really happened to him," contradicted Thally. "He was just scared by a white cow."

"There are no white cows in Cedarshore," declared the short lady. "But perhaps you had better explain, Beulah," and she turned toward the tall lady.

"Yes," was the reply. "Miss Duncan—Miss Bond," she said, formally, "I am Miss Beulah Spencer. This," and she indicated the short member, "is Miss Lucinda Lapwing and this," she bowed to the gentle-voiced delegate who bowed in acknowledgment, "is Miss Abigail Trotmore. We are all members of the Cedarshore Improvement Association and at a meeting we were appointed to visit you and kindly request you to go away and close up Rocky Cliff." And she closed her own mouth with a resounding snap.

"Close it up!" exclaimed Carol. "Why? We came here to—to——"

"To try to solve the mystery as many have tried before," interrupted Miss Spencer, apology in her voice for the interruption. "But it is unsolvable. Many have tried it. Each time some one comes here to live there are more and worse manifestations of some supernatural power. It is endangering the lives of those who stay here. Why, suppose that cupboard had fallen on one of you girls?" There was horror in her voice.

"Oh, you heard about that, did you?" asked Carol in mild sarcasm.

"Yes. Everyone in town has heard of it. And the disappearance of the Chinese dragon."

"It was a suit of Chinese armor," said Thally, gently corrective.

"The principle is the same," said Miss Spencer, rather frigidly. "It bears out my point—the points of all of us." She included her companions on her formal bow. "That, with the groans and moans, which are ancient history in a way, and the scaring of the colored boy—all this would seem to make it reasonable for you to grant our request—the request of our association, to close up the place and move away. We do not want to insist—indeed we have no right," she admitted. "It is just for the good of Cedarshore and your own good that we ask you—that we entreat you!" She was very much in earnest. Really she seemed frightened as did the other ladies, for, every now and then they gazed about as though in apprehension. Carol was glad that, so far, there had been no uncanny demonstrations during the day. They had all happened at night.

"What is your decision?" asked Miss Spencer after a moment's pause.

"I—well—I hardly know what to say," answered

Carol. "You see, we are here at my aunt's request —we are in duty bound to do all we can to solve the mystery. If we leave now——"

"You had better leave before it is too late!" interrupted Miss Lapwing.

"Yes, indeed," echoed her companions.

"What I can't understand," said Thally, "though this doesn't mean we don't appreciate your visit, is how our going away is going to better matters. The moans sounded before we came. Presumably they will continue after we go."

"Yes," admitted Miss Spencer, "but with you gone no one will know about them. With you here and rumors spreading every day in the village, there is a continual detriment to our community. If you close up the place, as it was closed some time before you came, there will be no publicity, so to speak, for the ghosts. It is your occupancy of Rocky Cliff that has created such a stir in town. If you will be so kind as to leave, all will be the same as before. Let the ghosts have Rocky Cliff. Your aunt couldn't get rid of them and neither could any of her tenants. The place is doomed!"

She seemed to shiver a little as did her companions at this broad declaration.

"Well," Carol said, "it is kind of you to think of us and we can appreciate your anxiety concerning the reputation of Cedarshore, but I understand these queer happenings have been going on for some time, so I can't see——"

"Yes, they have been going on for some time," said Miss Spencer, not really interrupting, for Carol had about finished. "But they are getting worse. It may soon be too late." Her voice was suddenly solemn. "That is all we have to say or to request," she concluded.

"Please do as we ask!" gently pleaded Miss Trotmore.

"It is for your own good," added Miss Lapwing.

To this Carol made answer: "We shall think it over. Thank you."

The three little, old, almost dried-up ladies took their formal leave, and were soon bobbing down the road.

"Well?" gasped Carol.

"Did you ever hear of such a thing in your life?" Thally wanted to know. "Can they be serious?"

"I should say they were. But so are we. Come on; it is time for your decision, Thally. Will you stay or go?"

"What are *you* going to do, Carol?"

"I am going to stay on—with Rachel—it is all I can do. I promised Aunt Isabel. I can't let her down. Since there seems to be no actual danger, Dad would never forgive me if I did. I must——"

Carol was interrupted by a sound—it was the sound of moans and groans coming from somewhere within or about the house, from the air above

or the ground below. She stopped—gasped—
looked at Thally whose hand went to her rapidly
beating heart.

The moans grew louder. It was the first time,
since the girls had come to Rocky Cliff that the
ghostly demonstrations had occurred in the day
time.

"Carol, this settles it!" exclaimed Thally with
unhidden excitement. "I can't stand it another
hour. I'm going to—go. I'm sorry to leave you
but I can't stand it!"

"I don't blame you. This is something new—
the groans by daylight. I don't know what it
means." Carol was like one stunned.

Rachel came running to the front door from her
kitchen.

"Did you hear them?" she asked.

"As if we could help it!" murmured Thally.
"Oh, listen!"

One groan crescendoed into a shriek.

"There's nobody out back, playing tricks," declared the housekeeper. "Nobody at the sides. I
looked."

"There is nobody here at the front," said Carol.
"Our visitors departed just in time to avoid fleeing
in terror. Well, Thally, I don't believe we can
solve this mystery. I'm willing to go home with
you. I'll explain to Aunt Isabel in a letter."

The groans and moans suddenly ceased as Carol

concluded.   Then, as the three stood on the fron
porch, still fearful and wondering, a boy on ;
bicycle came riding madly along the walk in fron
of the old house.   He had a yellow envelope in hi;
hand.

"Anybody named Duncan live here?" he callec
over the fence.

"Yes," Carol replied.   "I am Miss Duncan."

"Message for you—paid—sign there," and h
handed over to Carol the black oil-cloth coverec
book with the enveloped telegram.

Quickly she signed.   Quickly she opened the en
velope and quickly she read.

"It's a wired letter from Aunt Isabel," she tolc
Thally.   "Listen.   She says that her half-brother
Sim Rollinson, has been to see her.   He says h
hears she is not making profitable use of this plac
and that the people of Cedarshore have condemnec
it.   So he is going to claim it under the will—th
first of this month.   That is only about a week off
Aunt Isabel wants to know if we have found ou
about the mystery and can suggest some way o
clearing it up so she can either rent it or live her
herself.   She asks us to rush an answer.   Wha
shall I tell her, Thally?"

For several seconds Thally did not reply.   Ther
she straightened up, as though adjusting her shoul
ders for a new burden and said:

"Tell her we're staying on and we're going t

clear up this mystery. Wire her that everything is going to be all right."

"Thally, you're a dear!" said Carol a little chokingly. "I thought I could depend on you. Here, boy, wait a minute," for he was riding away. "I want to send an answer to this telegram."

CHAPTER XXIII

COULD IT BE!

GRINNING, yet with curious, half frightened looks back at the strange old house, the boy departed with Carol's telegram, having gladly accepted a ten cent tip.

"We're committed to it now, Carol," said Thally. "We've got to stay here. But I feel more determined when I think of our Warning Committee."

"Yes; so do I. You don't regret your brave decision, I'm sure of that."

"No!" Thally was screwing her courage to the sticking point. "But I do wish," she went on, "that we had some one to call on, other than Jensen. Carol, do you know I have what may be a fantastic theory."

"What is it?"

"That Jensen, or someone he knows about, is making these noises."

"Whyever would he do that?"

"Read that answer in that telegram," said Thally, pointing to the message from Aunt Isabel still in Carol's hand.

214

"You mean——"

"I mean your aunt's mean half-brother—you told me she said he was mean. As I understand it, he wants this place. He can't get it as long as your aunt lives here or can get some sort of an income from it. This she has not been able to do. And unless she does it by the first of the month she loses the place. Am I right?"

"Right as rain, as Cecy would say, were she here."

"Then take the next step. If Mr. Rollinson can prevent your aunt from living here or prevent any tenants from staying, his object is accomplished, as they say in books. Once your aunt loses her hold on the place, it comes to him, under the will. Now, is it beyond the stretch of our feeble imaginations to guess that Mr. Rollinson or some one in his pay —say Jensen—is the author of these strange noises?"

"But how do they do it?" asked Carol after a pause.

"That's what we've got to find out. But I am prepared to state my belief in the theory that the noises are of human origin. If they are and we can prove it, we don't need to fear ghosts. And that's what I've been dreading and fearing. But I'm changing my mind."

"So have I, in a way," Carol confessed, "though I hate to admit it I really have dreaded something —well, weird, at any rate."

"So if we have something human to combat," Thally went on, "it is simpler, isn't it?"

"Yes," Carol agreed, "if we can only prove that the manifestations are of human origin. But they are certainly elusive."

"That's our job from now on," said Thally. "And one other thing——"

"Just a moment," interrupted Carol. "Do you believe that the disappearance of the Chinese warrior was of *human origin?*"

"Most certainly. He didn't vanish into thin air. Though I admit I can't see how he got out of the closet," reasoned Thally.

"We'll take that up under the head of new business," Carol said, laughing a little. She was glad to note she could still laugh even a little.

Then they talked of the ladies committee waiting on them, but that made the girls more determined than ever not to be "side-tracked" as Carol put it.

"If someone had just stuck it out long ago it would be all over now," she declared, wisely.

"Exactly," agreed Thally. "But one thing we must do at once," she continued.

"What?" asked Carol.

"We must have a man here, Glenn, Ted or somebody, but they have just gone back home from camp. I don't trust Jensen any more, though I think he did tell the truth about the fallen cupboard. Now, whom can we get to guard us?"

As if in direct answer to Thally's question, at that moment a voice hailed the two girls. It came from the little shaded lane, which curled around in front of the old house. And the voice inquired:

"How do you do?"

Carol and Thally looked up to see strolling along, Barry Brennan and his sister.

"Oh, how nice of you to call!" cried Carol, running down to the gate to meet them. "Do come in! Is your leg all better?" she asked the young engineer eagerly.

"Almost, or I wouldn't have dared venture so far. Though I didn't walk up from Mrs. Ronnie's. We came as far as we could in our car and walked the rest of the way. It's a relief to get away from our boarding place." He was smiling happily and with his sister both were most welcome at that auspicious moment.

"We're so glad to see you!" murmured Thally as the two came up on the porch—the young scientist walking rather slowly.

"We meant to come before and return your visit," said Miss Brennan "but something always seemed to prevent it. Though perhaps you are busy just now," she quickly added, glancing at the telegram in Carol's hand.

"No. Oh, no indeed, and—Thally—I have the grandest idea!" she suddenly exclaimed.

"You have! What?"

"You were asking for a man—here he is!"

Rather dramatically Carol pointed at Barr
Brennan.

"If you will take me off the sick list—yes—per
haps," said the young engineer, smiling. "But
don't quite understand."

"Have you ever hunted ghosts?" asked Carol
impetuously.

"Ghosts?"

"At least ghostly noises," Carol went on
"Surely, living at Mrs. Ronnie's, as you have been
you must have heard the gossip about this place—
Moaning Cliff?"

"We have heard stories," admitted the sister
"but we didn't believe them."

"But there is some truth in them," murmured
Carol. "Let me tell you."

The whole story, from the very beginning, was
hastily told, down to the telegram from Aunt Isa
bel and the decision of the girls to stay and try
still further to solve the mystery.

"Now," concluded Carol, "you two are the an
swer to the prayers of two maidens—will you come
and visit here with us for a while—until the first
of the month? Can you? We'll make you com
fortable. I'm sure you'll like Rachel's cooking.
And if your plans will permit——"

"Oh, I still have some of my vacation left," said
the young engineer.

"But won't our coming here, on your kind invitation, put you out?" asked his sister.

"Not at all," Carol made haste to say. "We have lost two members of our party—my sister and her chum. They were frightened away. If you will, you can take their places. Please come!"

Brother and sister exchanged glances. Then Miss Brennan said:

"We might come on one condition. For I must admit that life at Mrs. Ronnie's—though she has been lovely to Barry in his crippled state—has been anything but ideal. I should love it here! But I must insist on one condition if we come. I think Barry will agree with me."

"Of course," he said, "without asking what, Jessie."

"I hope the condition isn't too hard," smiled Carol.

"Not at all. It is that you allow us to pay for our board as we have been doing at Mrs. Ronnie's," said Miss Brennan.

"Oh, no! I couldn't think of that!" exclaimed Carol. "You must come as guests."

"As paying guests!" smiled the young engineer's pretty sister.

Carol hesitated. Thally took advantage of the opening.

"Of course, Carol!" she cried. "It is just the thing. We can take their board money, if they insist, and give it to your aunt. Then she will be making profitable use of the place. It will defeat her scheming half-brother. Now, Carol, my love, we're going to rout out these human ghost-noise makers with the help of science, I hope you don't mind me calling you Science," she said, smiling at the young man.

"Not at all," he laughed.

And so at last the real work began.

CHAPTER XXIV

MIDNIGHT FLOOD

BARRY BRENNAN and his pretty sister took up their residence, as "paying guests," in Rocky Cliff next day. Barry, as he asked Carol and Thally to call him, insisted on paying the first week's board in advance.

"And I want a receipt," he laughed. "It may be useful if your aunt has to prove her contention, in a court of law, that she has made profitable use of her mansion. You can sign, Carol, as her agent."

"I shall. Thanks for the suggestion. But are you sure you and Jessie (they were all first-naming now) won't be frightened away by the ghosts? If you are I shall have to give you back the board money."

"No," Jessie said, "I am not easily frightened."

"And as for giving back the money," joked Barry, "I shall refuse to take it. Anyhow it would be forfeited if we left and you didn't put us out."

"Don't let that last bother you," said Thally. "We won't let you go, not to speak of putting you out."

So it had been arranged. The night before Barry

and Jessie came to lodge with Carol and Thally passed without so much as a ghostly whimper, for which the two girls, and Rachel, no less, were very grateful.

Then, when the Brennans came they all breathed easier.

"I have no doubt," the young engineer said, "that the sounds you have heard, and any other manifestations are due to natural causes or to human agencies. They always are."

"There speaks the scientist!" laughed Thally. It was such a relief to have a man there!

"Do be serious!" Carol begged. "This means a lot to all of us."

"We may all be serious enough—tonight!" Thally said, significantly.

"Is it so awful?" asked Jessie.

"Wait until you hear," Thally answered.

"Please tell us some more," begged Carol of Barry, like a child teasing for a story.

"Oh," the young man resumed, "about my theory, that all this," and he included the whole big house in a comprehensive gesture, "is due to natural or human causes. Of course human causes include natural, but natural does not always include human. Now, I'm not going to say anything more until I have had a look around the place by daylight. I understand all the sounds come at night?"

"Once they didn't," said Thally.

"Well, we'll go into that. I want to hear them

myself before I theorize any more.   And, as I said,
I want to look the place over."

"Including Jensen," said Thally, meaningly.

"Yes, Jensen.   As you say, he may be an agent
and doing some underhand work."

When Carol and Thally told Jessie and her
brother of the ladies committee call, that incident
seemed funnier than before.

"But it adds importance to the whole story,"
Barry pointed out.   "For if the reputation of this
place is so poor as to invite a protest there must
be something *very* wrong going on."

So the first day of the occupancy was devoted to
a careful inspection of the premises, and the
grounds outside, by the young engineer.   Before
doing this, however, he had Carol and Thally carefully describe all that had happened, how they had
investigated in the cellar and how they had found
nothing.   They told of the falling cupboard.   Always thorough, as scientists should be, Barry insisted on removing the structure from the corner
where Jensen had nailed it in place again and ex-
amining the back.   The young engineer had brought
with him a set of tools of various kinds, the uses
of some forming a puzzle to Carol and Thally.

"You wouldn't think Barry was on his vacation
when you look at the tools," laughed Jessie.

"It's a vacation for me to find a new kind of
work," said her brother.

He confirmed what Jensen had said about the

nails of the cupboard having rusted away so as to cause the fall when some heavy vibration, like a thunder clap, started it. The supports of the cupboard, too, were not strong enough until Jensen replaced them, Barry said.

"Now I'll look around outside," he announced to the girls "and later I'll have a go down cellar. Then we'll be all ready for the night's alarm."

"If one comes," said Carol.

"I hope it does!" declared Barry, boldly. "I should be disappointed if I wasn't honored with a manifestation now that I am here."

The girls were so relieved with such assurance, they even hoped themselves that Barry would have a chance to hear the noises.

He spent several hours wandering about the old house and grounds. He walked in the direction of Jensen's cottage, and was viewed by the caretaker in rather surly greeting before he came away.

"Did you discover anything?" Carol asked at lunch.

"Not yet. But I haven't finished. I still have the house and attic to explore."

"Need any help?" asked Thally, hopefully.

"Not help—but I like company," he said, rather pointedly as he smiled at her.

"Then we'll all come," Carol said, and they did, Jessie going into raptures over the antiques in the attic. But nothing more was found than the girls had seen themselves and this, in terms of the mystery, was distinctly zero.

"Now for the cellar!" Barry announced gaily, as he got a specially large flashlight from his kit of tools, together with some other pieces of apparatus. "There the secret lies, I am sure!"

But it was still a hidden secret at the end of more than an hour of close inspection of every part of the cellar, by the young engineer. He even listened along the walls with something like a big stethoscope, causing Thally to ask:

"How is the respiration of the old house, Doctor Brennan?"

"Perfectly normal," he answered, smiling.

The inspection was almost over, they were on their way back to the inside stairway ready to go up (Carol had reiterated what she had said about the noises being heard only at night except in the one instance), they had commented on the fact that the time of the night noises varied, when suddenly Barry stopped in front of what seemed to be a large square boxed-in corner. It ran from floor to ceiling.

"What's this?" he asked.

"I don't know," Carol said. "One of the supports of the first floor beams, I should say."

Barry tapped it with a hammer. A resounding hollow sound followed.

"No beams supported on this," he announced.

"It's a hollow, upright box. Sort of a dumb-waiter shaft, I should say. Do you mind if I open it, Carol?"

"Not at all. We must open up everything. Do you think the noises came from there?"

"I don't know. Please hold my light, Jessie. I'm going to operate!" he told Thally merrily.

It did not take him long to rip off a few boards. And then, in the gleam of the various electric torches was revealed another of the secrets of the mystery.

Staring out at the investigators from within the dark shaft, was the evil, grinning face of the Chinese warrior. His armor was somewhat disarranged and one edge of the pedestal was broken, giving him an odd, lurching position. But there he was!

"Oh, my gosh!" cried Thally.

"What an awful looking thing!" gasped Jessie. "No wonder you girls were nervous with this around."

"But it disappeared," Carol exclaimed. "How in the world did it get down here?"

"It fell from above," Barry said, stepping partly within the shaft and looking up with his light to aid him. "You said this Foo Chung, or whatever his name is, was stored away in a closet?"

"In the big, hall closet," Carol said.

"Then he broke his way through the closet floor and came down here to be in seclusion," Barry said.

(And when *he* laughed the echo surely was a merry warble.)

"But the closet floor is solid—not a hole in it," asserted Thally.

"Trap door, very likely," said the young engineer. "We'll have a look."

Not waiting to replace the boards he had removed from the sides of the shaft, he went up stairs, followed by the girls. A quick inspection of the closet by his trained eyes and hands showed that his first guess was right. The middle of the closet floor consisted of a trap door, so cleverly arranged and with such close-fitting joints that a casual look would not reveal the secret.

But Barry was unable to find out how the trap door operated. He pushed on it, sought a hidden spring and even stepped on it with one foot, bringing half his weight to bear, but the trap door would not spring down, as it undoubtedly had done when the Chinese warrior stood on it, and was dropped down through to the cellar.

"This door works by some device I can't quite discover yet," Barry said, coming out of the closet. "I'll find it later."

"After you discover the real ghost," suggested Carol.

"Yes," he laughed. "But I think what happened was this. Your Chinese friend was squarely upon the centre of the trap door. When the closet fell the jar of it operated the door. Or the closet, in pulling itself loose from the wall, may have operated the hidden spring. At any rate the trap was sprung, the armored figure, as we may call it, though there is no figure inside, dropped down through the trap which then sprang back into place like the trick door in a theatre stage."

"So simple as all that," murmured Thally, with a comical sigh.

"But why do you suppose," asked Jessie, "there is such a thing as a trap door in a closet leading down into an abandoned dumb-waiter shaft?"

"Perhaps Carol's kidnapped miller ancestor, mindful of his former experience, wanted a way of quick escape in sudden danger," said Barry.

"I must ask Aunt Isabel about that," Carol said. "I never heard her mention it. And I'm glad we never used that old dingy closet."

"So am I," said Thally. "Just think! Suppose one of us had stepped on that trap door and had fallen through!"

"There was little danger, I think," said Barry. "It needed the working of the hidden spring or catch to let the trap fall. Just your weight on it wouldn't do it. Well, we've found out something, anyhow."

"A lot, I think," said Carol.

"And if you can only discover who is doing that mournful moaning we'll have cleared up the mystery," said Thally. She showed plainly she was tired of waiting for *that* to happen.

"I'll do my best," the young man promised.

They did not take the trouble to move the Chinese warrior from the shaft where he leaned, leering and lop-sided against the walls.

"Serves him right for being so ugly," Thally said.

The inspection of the grounds and the house by the investigating party, headed by Barry, was over late in the afternoon. Then came a restful walk out upon the cliff and the young engineer showed much interest in the quicksands. He said he planned to test them, but at a safe distance, with a bag weighted with stones, to resemble a human body.

"How horrible!" breathed Thally.

"Nothing scientific is horrible," Barry insisted politely.

They sat up later that night, making really quite a little party of it. The housekeeper locked up the house as usual, not even delegating this task to Barry who wanted to do it. Then they went to bed, Barry being given the room Cecy had lately occupied, while his sister was in the one Rosie had abandoned.

It must have been shortly after midnight the usual manifestations began. First there was a low hum or vibration, quickly increasing to agonized moans and increasing into shrill shrieks.

"There it is!" shouted Thally from her room.

"Barry! Barry!" his sister called.

"Don't be afraid!" Carol reassured her, coming out into the hall. "Nothing ever really happens— I mean we don't see anything and no one has ever been hurt."

"You mean nothing ever happens after all those blood-curdling groans?" asked Jessie. "Oh, they're awful! I don't see how you ever stood them!"

"I'm not going to stand it any more!" declared Thally. "If we don't find out what this means I'm off for home in the morning."

"And I'll not hold you back!" said Carol, reasonably enough.

Barry came out of his room in a blue bathrobe and carrying a big flashlight.

"Is this it?" he asked with a cheerful smile.

"Yes," Carol said. "Pretty terrible, isn't it?"

"Well, it isn't exactly something to induce sleep," he admitted. "But we'll have a look." He switched on his large, powerful flashlight, the sort used by police and firemen answering a midnight alarm. Then they all started the parade downstairs, Carol switching on the illumination from the upper hall as she reached it. As they walked toward the inside cellar door a shadowy figure was seen moving about.

"Look!" cried Thally. "There it is! Oh!"

Even Carol was alarmed for a moment, but a second later she saw it was Rachel who had gone down the back stairs. The housekeeper was already opening the cellar door with her usual efficiency. As the door swung back the sounds of moans, shrieks and cries seemed to increase. And then Rachel, with fear in her voice exclaimed:

"The cellar is full of water! It's a flood! We'll all be drowned in our beds!" Which last statement was slightly exaggerated. But not the other. Barry took one look down into the cellar, his flashlight focused there, then he cried:

"It's a flood, all right, and rising fast!"

CHAPTER XXV

AUNT ISABEL WINS

CROWDED back of Barry, the girls looked down upon a strange scene. The cellar was filled with swirling water that gurgled and whispered above the moans and groans which, however, to the now trained ears of Carol and Thally, were dying away.

"It's as though the rising water had drowned the ghost," Thally said, tragically.

"Oh, how terrible!" murmured Jessie, impulsively clinging to Carol.

"Now, girls, don't get nervous," Barry warned with a laugh. "This flood is just a manifestation of nature. It's right in my line of business and I'm going to investigate. Probably it's only a broken waterpipe."

"But do you think water pipes made the groans?" challenged Thally.

"Too soon to tell yet. I'm going down there and find out. Have you any lighting system down cellar, Carol?"

"Oh, yes." She switched on the lights which were all in the ceiling and so, not yet affected by the rising waters.

"Fine! Be with you in a second," said Barry turning to go back up stairs.

"What's he going to do?" Thally asked Jessie.

"I don't know. He has some plan," she answered.

Soon Barry came hurrying back attired in his bathing suit. He handed his big flashlight to his sister remarking:

"Can't use that down there. It would short-circuit in the wet. But the cellar lights will be enough. Now don't worry. I'm a good swimmer. I'll be all right."

As he started down the stairs, where the water was now half-way up, Carol noticed that Barry had, slung around his neck, the rubber tubes of what appeared to be a big stethoscope. He stepped down into the swirling waters, all his movements being easily seen in the illumination of the overhead bulbs, and began to wade around. Then he was lost to sight being out of range of those observing him from the head of the cellar steps.

"Oh!" gasped Thally. "Suppose he doesn't come back!"

"Stop it!" sharply ordered Carol. "This is no baby class."

"You needn't worry about Barry," said his sister. "He once swam into a cave, diving down beneath the rocky entrance that was below water level. He is very daring. And his leg is not strained now, you know."

Tense moments passed.   Then more tense seconds.   Finally the minutes seemed like hours to the girls watching.   Every now and then low agonizing moans would come from the cellar and they could hear Barry sloshing around.

Suddenly the girls and the housekeeper were startled by a scream so shrill and piercing as to cause them all to fairly jump.

"That's the worst I ever heard!" cried Thally. "Be careful Barry!" she called.

"Yes," Carol had to admit.   "That is awful."

Following that shrill, awful shriek came an intense silence.   And then, a blessed relief to the watchers and listeners, came the voice of Barry as he shouted:

"I've found it!"

"What, the ghost—the noise-maker?" demanded Carol instantly alert.

"No, but the cause of the flood and a way to cure it.   At least a way to lower the water, though it will still come in.   But I think the outlet will be large enough to take care of it," he added, even in that exciting moment, when it was very difficult to make himself heard.

Then the girls noticed that the water was no longer rising.   It quickly began to subside, and a loud gurgle, as when the plug is pulled out of a full bathtub, proclaimed that the outlet was open.

Then again came a groan; several of them though not so loud and terrifying as at first.   Followed another period of silence. The water was going down fast. Barry came back toward the steps, wading more easily this time. Carol and the others saw that he held his stethoscope in his hands. They saw him apply the cup-shaped end of it to a certain part of the cellar wall near the steps. Into his ears the young engineer put the two nipples.

As he stood there, listening, several moans resounded.

Listening, as a doctor might to the breathing of his patient, Barry suddenly stepped back, pulled the nipples from his ears and triumphantly exclaimed:

"I've found it!"

"The ghost?" asked Carol.

"If you want to call it that—yes. But I've found out what has caused the moans."

"What?" they all demanded, even Rachel adding her voice.

"Compressed air," was Barry's answer.

"Compressed air?" faltered Carol. "What can that mean?"

"Let him come up! Come on up, Barry!" Thally ordered, and soon the hero of the hour was with them in the kitchen, dripping wet. But Rachel said it was all right she was going to scrub in the morning anyhow.

Then he told them: "Air is compressed in hollow tubes and passages of the rocky foundation of this old house. The air is compressed by the action of some underground stream. Just where the stream is I don't know yet, but I'll find out. I think it runs under the cellar and may account for the flood. But there is no doubt but that the water seeping into the rocky holes and tubes, compressed the air. In escaping it whistled, moaned, groaned and shrieked just as happens to a compressed air whistle or to the big pipes of an organ."

The pipe organ simile was perfectly understandable to Carol and Thally. They remembered the big pipe organ that figured in another mystery— the first story of Melody Lane.

"And is that what caused the moans?" asked Jessie.

"Yes. I am quite sure of it," her brother answered. "I listened through this enlarged stethoscope of mine," and he swung the instrument to and fro. "It gave me a close-up of what is going on back of the cellar wall, just as a doctor can hear through the chest walls of his patients. Depend on it, compressed air has been playing all these tricks, compressed air and an underground stream working in conjunction," he concluded.

"It's a wonder nobody ever found it before," said Rachel, rather sharply.

"Probably nobody ever thought to look for this before," said Barry as he shook himself like a big wet dog and the girls squealed as they escaped the shower.

"Oh, I'm so glad it's all over," Thally said.

"Won't your Aunt Isabel be too tickled for words, Carol?" Thally asked.

"Yes, Aunt Isabel wins and she can keep the property, for with the noises gone it will no longer be Moaning Cliff. There will be no terror here and she can live here herself or rent it. That mean half-brother of hers can't get it away from her. Oh, it's just wonderful. We can't thank you enough, Barry."

"Don't try. I had a lot of fun solving this. Really it was very simple. But I'll get a kick out of it when I write an article for our engineering paper. I'll make my summer vacation expenses, including my doctor's bill, out of the story," he triumphantly declared.

"That will be fine!" said Thally. "The old mill disabled you but the old house mystery paid you back," she intoned dramatically.

"That's right," admitted Barry.

"But what about the flood?" asked Carol. "Where did the water come from and how did you get rid of it?"

"The water came in through a break in the back cellar wall," Barry said. "I could see where it was pouring in. Probably the underground stream is higher than usual now and, after long years, the cellar wall probably weakened and gave way. It must have happened before this time, as I found an outlet valve, or gate, operated by what we call a worm gear, high up on the front cellar wall. I turned the hand wheel and the worm gear opened the valve, so that the water is running out faster than it is running in. You won't be really flooded now," he assured them.

"Thank goodness for that!" murmured Rachel. "I can't bear a flood in my kitchen."

They laughed at her—laughed joyously for the first time in a long while. Then, when Barry had changed into his dry pajamas and bath robe and they were all sitting in the wee, small hours of the morning in the big living room, Carol asked:

"But if the underground stream compressed the air in holes and passages of the rocky ground on which this house is built, how can the groans be stopped, Barry?"

"By changing the course of the underground stream. It will take some digging, but it can be done. Just an engineering problem."

"I wish all problems were as simple as that," said Thally with a happy sigh. "It just doesn't seem possible."

They talked and talked. Somehow it was hard to give up the old ghost idea, it had been so real, so true. But they went to bed at last, Barry promising in the morning to take them with him to discover where the source of the underground stream might be, and to trace it, if possible, to its violent point of energy under the house.

This was done after a rather late breakfast, for

they all slept soundly after the big discovery and the falling of the flood water. It did not take the young engineer long to trace the source of the underground stream to the headwaters of Clam Creek, which served not only, in times past, to operate the grist mill but, even now, worked the machinery for a small tin can factory about three miles back in the country from Rocky Ledge.

The same stream operated the can factory and formerly the grist mill and after giving this service, it flowed into the bay near the quicksands. Barry found where the stream divided, part of it flowing into a rocky glen where it dropped down through a great hole and was lost to view.

"From here," he told the girls, pointing it out to them, "the stream flows underground. It must have been flowing thus for many years and, in the course of time, has honeycombed the underlying rock strata with many holes. It was these holes, beneath the cellar floor of the old house, and some back of the side walls, that made such mournful music."

"Did you ever hear of such a thing before?" asked Thally. "I mean, is there any record of such weird sounds coming out of holes in a rock?"

"Oh, yes," said Barry. "I remember reading in the book 'Tom Brown at Rugby' how Tom goes to an inn near the Great White Horse. Back of the hotel bar was a great stone, part of the walls of the place. In that rock is a hole. When the inn-keeper put his mouth to the hole and blew in, thus compressing the air as the water compressed it here, a most mournful wail came forth, much to the amazement of young Tom Brown."

"How wonderful!" exclaimed Carol.

"Well, ain't nature wonderful?" chuckled Barry.

"Barry!" remonstrated his sister, but her pride in him was perfectly plain to all.

"And you are sure the moans can be stopped?" Thally asked.

"Positive—just by changing the course of this stream here.   Change it from an underground brook into an upper one and the noises will end."

"I must telegraph Aunt Isabel," Carol said.

"But what I can't understand," said Thally, "is why the noises sounded only at night."

"We heard them once in the daytime," Carol said.

"Yes, that's so."   They looked to Barry for an explanation.

"That, too, is simple," he said.   "I made some inquiries at the tin can factory while you girls were outside picking flowers.   The factory runs only during the day and uses so much water from the stream for its turbine wheel, that little was left to flow in the underground channel and so compress the howling air.   At night the factory closes. Then the water accumulates, not being used in the turbine shaft and it fills the underground passages. I have no doubt that on the day in question you will find that the mill was shut down for repairs."

Later this was found to be so. Also the reason no noises were overheard during daylight hours on Sunday, was because on Sundays the engineer of the mill usually kept the water flowing into the turbine shaft to make repairs about the place which he was unable to do when the machinery was in operation.

"Well, so that's the end of the mystery," remarked Carol as they went back to Rocky Cliff.

"The only one we really didn't solve all by ourselves," said Thally, a little grudgingly.

"Oh, but I think you Melody Lane girls are—well fearless at any rate," said Jessie. "And if you hadn't rescued Barry the time he fell off the wheel the mystery might not yet be solved. So, really, you did it after all."

"Won't Glenn and Ted be surprised?" Carol reasoned.

"There's one thing we haven't found out," said Thally as they neared the old house.

"What?" asked Barry.

"The ghost that scared poor little Toledo."

"Well, whatever it was had nothing to do with the noises in the cellar," Barry explained. "And I believe either the boy imagined he saw something or it was just some white animal—a cow."

"Everyone in Cedarshore says there are no white cows here," declared Carol.

"Well, white horse then," Barry laughed. "I'm not particular." But the girls were and they never stopped until a few days later they found that it was a white horse that had escaped from a pasture not far away, that had been the cause of Toledo's fright.

"And we even blamed poor Jensen and his wife," bemoaned Thally.

"And I thought old Uncle Sim was running the ghost show," added Carol.

"Well, I suppose now we can go back to Melody Lane with banners flying," said Thally a few days after all the excitement had subsided.

"Yes," Carol agreed. "We have, as the books say, accomplished our purpose."

"Was your aunt pleased?"

"Oh, yes. Didn't I show you her telegram in answer to mine? She says she'll thank us properly later and, characteristic of her, she adds to her wire. 'As for Sim, we showed him a thing or two.'"

Thally could laugh like her old self now, and she was doing just that.

"And just hear this, she authorized us," Carol went on, "to have Barry engage men to change the course of the underground stream so the noises will be heard no more, and there will be no further danger of floods. But, best of all, Aunt Isabel says she has accepted an offer to rent Rocky Cliff on a long lease to another doctor who is going to make a rest cure of it."

"His patients can get some rest now that the noisy ghosts are silent," said Thally.

"Yes," Carol agreed. "And, believe me, this is the last mystery I'm going to be mixed up with, that is if I can keep clear of them, of course."

But Melody Lane mysteries did not end with the solution of that at Moaning Cliff, and certainly Carol Duncan and her chums would have to see them through, if they promised as much interest and adventure as the others had provided.

The promise was very thoroughly borne out, as is told in the next volume of this series, "The Dragon of the Hills."

This is the story of an enchanting and subtle perfume, bearing that baffling label. It turned the girls' little tea shop into an emporium of exciting mystery and drama.

THE END

MELODY LANE
MYSTERY STORIES
By LILIAN GARIS

Thrills, secrets, ghosts—adventures that will fascinate you seem to surround pretty Carol Duncan. A vivid, plucky girl, her cleverness at solving mysteries will captivate and thrill every mystery fan.

THE GHOST OF MELODY LANE
Three people see the "ghost" that wanders in the grove carrying a waxy white rose. And in the end Carol finds the rose and the ghost too!

THE FORBIDDEN TRAIL
Carol has several bad frights before she clears up the mystery that keeps the family at Splatter Castle unhappy and afraid.

THE TOWER SECRET
The winking lights from the old tower defy explanation. Had the engaging circus family anything to do with them?

THE WILD WARNING
What power did the strange, wild warning in the woods have over Polly Flinders? Carol brings happiness to three families when she solves this mystery.

THE TERROR AT MOANING CLIFF
Carol finally tracks the uncanny "haunts" in the great, bleak house on "moaning cliff" to their source.

THE DRAGON OF THE HILLS
When Carol runs a tea shop for a friend, a baffling mystery comes to her with her first customer.

THE MYSTERY OF STINGYMAN'S ALLEY
An adorable child is left at the day nursery where Carol works—who are all the mysterious people trying to claim her?

THE SECRET OF THE KASHMIR SHAWL
A sequel to "The Wild Warning"
A shawl brought from Egypt brings with it an absorbing mystery which Cecy, with the aid of Polly Flinders, finally solves.

GROSSET & DUNLAP : *Publishers* : NEW YORK

THE CAROLYN WELLS
BOOKS FOR GIRLS

Fresh, spirited stories that the modern small girl will take to her heart these well known books by a famous author have won an important place in the field of juvenile fiction.

THE FAMOUS "PATTY" BOOKS

Patty Fairfield	Patty's Motor Car
Patty at Home	Patty's Butterfly Days
Patty in the City	Patty's Social Season
Patty's Summer Days	Patty's Suitors
Patty in Paris	Patty's Romance
Patty's Friend	Patty's Fortune
Patty's Pleasure Trip	Patty Blossom
Patty's Success	Patty — Bride

Patty and Azalea

THE MARJORIE BOOKS

Marjorie's Vacation	Marjorie in Command
Marjorie's Busy Days	Marjorie's Maytime
Marjorie's New Friend	Marjorie at Seacote

TWO LITTLE WOMEN SERIES

Two Little Women
Two Little Women and Treasure House
Two Little Women on a Holiday

DORRANCE SERIES

The Dorrance Domain
Dorrance Doings

GROSSET & DUNLAP : *Publishers* : NEW YORK

Stories of Fun and Friendship

THE MAIDA BOOKS
by INEZ HAYNES IRWIN

MAIDA'S LITTLE SHOP

In a darling little shop of her own Maida makes many friends with the school children who buy her fascinating wares.

MAIDA'S LITTLE HOUSE

All of her friends spend a happy summer in Maida's perfect little house that has everything a child could wish for.

MAIDA'S LITTLE SCHOOL

Three delightful grownups come to visit and the children study many subjects without knowing that they are really "going to school."

MAIDA'S LITTLE ISLAND

Great is the joy of the Big Eight when Maida's father takes them for a vacation to *Spectacles*, where exploring the island provides endless fun and many thrilling adventures.

MAIDA'S LITTLE CAMP

High in the Adirondacks the four boys and four girls of the Big Eight spend a glorious month of fun and discovery.

GROSSET & DUNLAP : *Publishers* : NEW YORK

THE DANA GIRLS
MYSTERY STORIES

by Carolyn Keene

Author of the

NANCY DREW MYSTERY STORIES

Impetuous, delightful Jean Dana and her charming
serious-minded sister, Louise, find themselves in the midst
of several mysteries when they attempt to aid people who
are in trouble. There are thrilling moments as the girls
follow up clue after clue in an endeavor to untangle the
knotty problems in which they become enmeshed.

BY THE LIGHT OF THE STUDY LAMP

THE SECRET AT LONE TREE COTTAGE

IN THE SHADOW OF THE TOWER

A THREE-CORNERED MYSTERY

THE SECRET AT THE HERMITAGE

THE CIRCLE OF FOOTPRINTS

THE MYSTERY OF THE LOCKED ROOM

THE CLUE IN THE COBWEBS

THE SECRET AT THE GATEHOUSE

GROSSET & DUNLAP

Publishers   NEW YORK

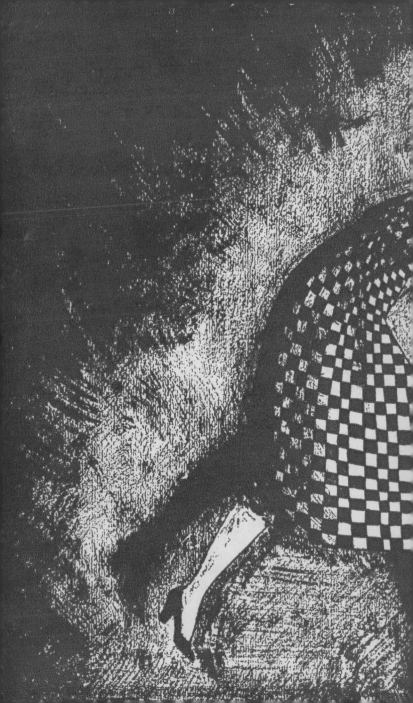